Tom Darling was born in Oxford in 1978.
He has an M.Phil. from Trinity College, Dublin.

www.tomdarling.com

SUMMER

Tom Darling

ABACUS

First published in Great Britain in 2012 by Abacus
This paperback edition published in 2013 by Abacus

A CIP catalogue record for this book
is available from the British Library.

ISBN 978-0-349-00001-5

Typeset in Sabon by M Rules
Printed and bound in Great Britain by
Clays Ltd, St Ives plc

Papers used by Abacus are from well-managed forests
and other responsible sources.

MIX
Paper from
responsible sources
FSC® C104740

Abacus
An imprint of
Little, Brown Book Group
100 Victoria Embankment
London EC4Y 0DY

An Hachette UK Company
www.hachette.co.uk

www.littlebrown.co.uk

For Diane

PART ONE

1

Dawn. Night poured into day, the sun rising quickly until its light crept into even the furthest corners. At the first heat the grains of barley in the fields around the farm clicked and cracked as the dew dried, like millions of waking insects. Beneath the roof of the milking parlour a quick-eyed wood-pigeon shifted at the change, ruffling her feathers and arranging herself closer still over her two eggs. For a time she watched the first flies of the day as they buzzed sleepily around her, before tucking her head back in and settling into her own warmth.

The children arrived soon after midday. The car that brought them stayed only as long as it took to unload their luggage, and of that there was very little: just two identical cases, one for each child. The children were themselves alike.

A glance was all that was needed to match the high eyebrows, the sharp noses and chins, the faintly jutting ears and nutmeg hair.

At first it was only the length of hair that revealed one of them to be a girl. But, if one looked closer, as the old man did now, standing in the farmyard with the dust from the departed car settling around them, it was clear to see. Long lashes shaded the girl's eyes, and the shape of her body beneath her clothes gave away the beginnings of womanhood. The girl's brother, meanwhile, showed no signs of an end to childhood. Half a foot shorter than his sister, his face was still all boy, his cheeks plump and smooth.

Together they stood, nearly touching at the shoulder. The journey had been a long one. They both felt the urge to stretch, but neither did so. They understood that, under the eyes of the old man, something like stretching would have been overly frivolous for such an occasion. They knew what was expected of them; their roles had been made clear. So, instead of stretching, they remained as motionless as possible and awaited instruction.

To the east of the farm a brook ran between an expanse of meadows, a silvery hairline crack in the otherwise perfect green. Beds of watercress flourished in the margins. Dragonflies flew in tandem as they mated. They paused, then moved on again. Back at the farm the old man led the boy and the girl inside, and up to the room that would be theirs.

*

The boy yawned. He'd slept little the night before, and hardly at all in the car, and he was tired. He rubbed at his right hand, which was swollen and flushed a deep and itchy red from carrying his case up the steep flight of stairs.

The girl eyed the shut door. Over the years the wooden panels had dried out and cracked, and she could see clear through. After the rush of the motorway and the blur of passing hedges everything was very still. She took out her mobile phone and when she saw its black screen she remembered. Finding the charger in her bag she plugged it in and turned it on. While she waited for it to start up, she listened. The boy was sitting on his bed, moving backwards and forwards and making the springs squeak.

'Shush a second, would you?'

He stopped and looked at her. 'Why?'

She gestured vaguely at the window. 'Just listen.'

'It's birds,' said the boy matter-of-factly after a few seconds. 'It's birds tweeting.'

The greeting tone sounded from the mobile. The girl looked at the brightly lit screen, waiting for it to find a signal.

'It's birds *and* your phone,' said the boy, '*both* of them tweeting.'

'Be quiet, would you, Billy?' She looked again at the screen.

The boy's face changed. Billy was his mother's nickname for him. Recently Grace had started to use it too, and when she did it made him feel funny, like his stomach and all his insides were pushing upwards into his chest.

He's right, thought Grace, there's nothing but birds. And then she realised that it was exactly this that she had heard, this lack of anything else. No cars, no buses, no sirens; not even the distant hum of a passing plane. She gave her phone one last hopeful look. Her heart sank.

She lifted her case onto the sun-bleached blanket on the bed. The catch snapped open, and there were her things. They were so abruptly familiar that it made her want to cry.

'Why are you doing that?' asked Billy.

She flicked her hair from her face and looked at him.

'Because we need to unpack our things. This is—'

He shook his head. 'Not that – I know that. I mean why are you calling me Billy? You never did before.'

She hesitated, feeling her own stomach starting to push upwards. She thought for a while for something to tell him, something helpful. When that didn't work she tried to imagine what her mother would say. In the end she shrugged and said, 'I don't know.' But she did know, and she suddenly felt bad for lying to her little brother, so she added, 'I suppose I just like saying it,' which was at least true.

The day inched on. In the heat nothing stirred, and it was early evening before the air began to cool, as though even the heat was too stifled by itself to move on. In the farmhouse the old man waited for the children to come downstairs.

When they didn't appear he thought to check on them, and he heaved himself to his feet.

He was halfway to the door when a memory made him pause. It was of the last time he had heard a child's voice coming from the room above. He stayed as he was, listening as though caught in a daydream, and then he did something he'd only rarely done before. Going over to the modest bureau that occupied one corner of the room, he began opening and shutting the drawers. It was here that Margaret had used to do the farm accounts; he could still picture her bent over with concentration as first she drew the columns and then wrote out the numbers within them. It had been one of the few corners of the farm that had been hers alone, and even now, years later, to go through the drawers felt like an intrusion, so he searched quickly.

He worked his way from the bottom up, knowing all the while that it was the top drawer he was interested in. A brass keyhole sat squarely at its centre, set into the wood, this the only lock there was on the whole bureau. Taking a bunch of keys from his pocket he selected one and opened it. From within he lifted out a shallow box made from cardboard.

Inside he found what he was looking for: a dozen or so photographs that made his heart feel heavy inside him. He studied one after the other, moving the thin pieces of paper from hand to hand before placing them back in the drawer. One, however, he kept, and he held it out before him, peering at it through his glasses. The girl in the picture stared back at him. Immediately he wanted go upstairs and hold it up beside the children and compare the likeness. Again he wondered if he shouldn't go up and check on them, and he found himself wishing that Margaret was there to guide him.

He walked through to the kitchen. Fetching some bread and butter and a jar of honey from the cupboards, together with some plates, he laid everything out on the table. He stood and looked down at it all. He thought to call them, but still he stayed as he was, unmoving. There's no use hurrying them, he told himself. There's plenty of time for all that.

He returned to his chair, which creaked as he settled into it. A small dog, a terrier, waited with him, its one unbroken ear pricking at the sounds that came from above. Its coat matched its master's white hair, and soon after the old man's head nodded and bowed, it stretched out its short legs and invited sleep to take it too.

Lynn and Michael Hooper spent the morning of the day it happened buying wetsuits for their two children. It was a trip Michael felt they shouldn't have had to make: having discovered a week beforehand that their local supermarket stocked wetsuits so cheap that he was considering buying one for himself, he had seized the opportunity to save yet more money and had taken his offspring for some pre-holiday shopping. William was easy: the second suit he tried fitted perfectly. But Grace was another matter altogether.

After her usual speech about supermarkets being environmentally unfriendly, which she proved by finding the tag ('See? Made in China. By children probably, which is why they're so cheap.' 'Oh come on,' Michael had replied, rolling his eyes, 'we're already not going abroad because of you. How about giving it a rest for a minute?') she then proceeded to struggle in and out of six or seven different suits. With the embarrassment of repeatedly standing before her father in such revealing garments fast turning to shame, it became apparent that her body occupied precisely that middle ground between girl and woman. It was her breasts that were the problem, and for Grace, whose relationship with her body was already under strain thanks to the changes that were occurring (some days she struggled to hide her pleasure when she detected the envy in the other girls; on other days she just wanted to hide), the sight of herself in the mirror was almost more than she could bear. The suits that fitted snugly around her hips made no allowances for what was further up, and when (sometimes it was if) she got the zip done up, her two breasts became one, squashed against her ribs in an unsightly lump. Alternatively, those suits whose upper contours matched her own sat baggily around her bottom, as though something was missing. There's no way around it, she thought as she looked in the mirror and steeled herself for her father's clumsily diluted comments, I'm not as I should be. If I was, one of these would fit and we could go home, and the shame of all this –

of shopping for wetsuits in a supermarket, of standing before my own father again and again in perhaps the most unflattering things ever devised – would be over. And more than that, she thought, taking one last glance at her mono-breast, I could still look forward to spending a week on a beach learning to surf.

And so when, instead of accepting that the manufacturers simply hadn't catered for his daughter's shape, and that there might be a reason besides their origins that these wetsuits were so cheap, Michael Hooper cheerfully nodded to indicate that their search had been fruitful, Grace said nothing. Back in the changing room she struggled out of the wetsuit, her skin clammy from the ordeal and beginning to squeak against the rubber. When she re-emerged her father was trying to persuade William to take his wetsuit off; after half an hour his face was starting to go the same shade of red it did on very cold winter mornings. This was still going on ('Yes, but what *I'm* saying is that I can't pay for it with you still inside it' – this from a man clearly used to having to bargain with his nine-year-old son – 'You can put it straight back on when we get home') when Dan Chapman, a boy in the year above her at St Siskins, and so far the only person to have moved her in a way that she couldn't describe, strolled by. She prayed that the sight of her younger brother being peeled out of a wetsuit yards from the bakery section was enough to distract attention away from her. For a time it looked hopeful. But five minutes later, with the checkout

10

girl holding the wetsuits aloft for all to see as she hunted about for the barcode, there he was again, this time with two friends in tow. Catching sight of her and then the wetsuit (it was as if her own body was being held up for inspection) the corners of their mouths turned collectively upwards. Grace stared back at them, and when Dan Chapman turned and said something to the others, she felt the heat at her cheeks. As the automatic doors swept open before them the sound of their laughter reached her, and the horror was complete.

Less than a week later, Grace was once again trying on wetsuits. This time, however, she was a quarter of a mile from the sea, and as if to prove it there was sand on the floor beneath her feet. Her mother, a former triathlete – once a county champion and twice runner-up – had known exactly what was needed. The shop assistant, a pretty girl whom Grace could tell was more used to dealing with a relaxed sort of customer, wisely let this square-shouldered woman take the lead in picking out a wetsuit for her daughter, only offering a few choice words of advice when it was asked for. Meanwhile Grace's father waited outside in the car. She knew there had been a row because nothing had been said. She knew what that kind of silence meant.

She heard her mother beyond the curtain. 'Billy, darling, please take those off; they're much too big for you and you'll only trip and break something.' There was a shuffling noise (What did he have on? Was it flippers?) followed by the brisk, bright sound of the shop assistant's flip-flops. The zip slid smoothly up the length of Grace's back, tracing her spine like a finger. She fastened the Velcro tab at her neck and looked in the mirror. It was a perfect fit, so perfect that she lingered awhile, turning to look at herself from different angles. Unlike before, the rubber of this suit seemed to be on her side, to know instinctively how to make the best of her curves. At five times the price of the one currently lying on her bed back at the cottage, it occurred to her that perhaps it was this innate intelligence that you were paying for. She turned side-on again. Starting from her feet she ran her eyes up, feeling a prick of pride at where the slenderness gave way to shape. She thought of Dan Chapman, and imagined it was his eyes that were seeing this, but even as she tried to picture him she found his image was blurred and indistinct. Now that she was here by the sea, where there was sun, sand and boys who surfed, Dan Chapman and his laughing friends no longer seemed important.

The surfers were generally to be found at Briscombe Bay. No more than a tiny indentation in the coastline, the bay was the result of a mix of rock. Over the centuries the softer stone between two headlands of the more resilient sandstone had been eroded. Two rocks remained in the bay itself, rearing out of the water a hundred yards offshore, one five times the size of the other. Although they looked to be unconnected, and were known locally as David and Goliath, the lowest spring tides revealed them to be part of the same reef.

It was this that drew the surfers, and in turn had persuaded the Hoopers to rent a cottage just a short walk away through sand-dunes prickly with coarse grass.

And so it was that an hour later, with the rubbery smell of new wetsuit intensifying around them from the heat of their bodies, Grace and William left their parents high up the beach and threaded their way through the other holiday-makers towards the sea. Their instructor, a balding man called Tim – who to Grace's disappointment and her parents' quiet delight was at least forty-five – showed them the basic technique. It was half an hour before they even got wet, but when they did Grace quickly discovered a natural aptitude for detecting the moment when the wave took hold of the board and she could spring to her feet; with a sense of balance it was generally accepted that she had inherited from her mother, she was soon surfing. I can do it, she said to herself with exhilaration after another successful take-off, the taste of salt strong in her mouth, I can surf!

Her brother found it less easy; his balance just wasn't there. Lying flat on his front and holding on to the sides of the board was the only time he felt remotely secure; the minute he started paddling his little ship lost all stability. Time and again he was tipped off the side, first one way, and then as he tried to compensate, the other. Each time he scrambled back on, coughing from the water he'd swallowed, his hands soon white again from the effort of holding on.

13

The instructor thought he'd give up. When they found it that hard they usually did. But when it became clear that the boy was either too determined to admit defeat, or was simply used to finding things difficult, he waved Grace in.

'Well done – you're a natural,' he called out as she approached through the surf, her board tucked under her arm. She smiled and glanced up the beach to see if her parents had been watching. Her father waved; next to him her mother made an exaggerated clapping motion above her head.

'I love it,' she said, still a little out of breath.

'You can catch them while they're still clean if you get further out.'

She looked beyond where the waves broke. Several surfers were out there already, some sitting astride their boards.

'Think you can manage it? I need to stay here with your brother.'

Together they watched as a small wave met his board side-on and turned him over only a few feet from them. She nodded.

'Okay then. You'll probably find it a bit tough to go straight out through the breakers, but there's a small rip that runs past the far rock. Walk down there and paddle into it and it'll take you out – don't worry, it peters out when it meets the deeper water – and then paddle back across to where the others are. Remember, don't try to fight the water, and if you get dumped,' he held his hands over his head to demonstrate, 'watch your head on your board. Those fins are sharp.'

She set off down the beach. Knowing her parents would be watching her, for once she enjoyed her self-consciousness. There too was the pleasure of discovering that she'd been right, that they didn't need to go abroad to enjoy their summer holiday. She worked it out in her head as she'd already done many times before: they were four people, so that was eight flights in all she had prevented. The Hooper family carbon footprint was that much smaller because of her.

The sand was hard beneath her feet, and the wetsuit made her body feel taut and powerful. But it was hard going: the wind had picked up, and now and then a gust caught the surfboard and nearly spun her around. It was a relief when she waded into the sea and was able to lie the board down, beyond the wind's reach. The rest was easy. The water was strangely calm, and as she paddled out she found she had the company of two other surfers. When she reached the rock – David, the smaller one – and the current took hold, she was glad of their smiles. The three of them swept along together, heading for the open sea.

The instructor was one of the few who saw it coming. In an instant he had the boy lifted out of the shallows and bundled up the beach. The first thing most people were aware of was the sound of rushing water; by the time they looked up the reef was already foaming from the first wave. Behind the white water the sea looked deeper and darker than before. What happened then was nearly magical. The light-heartedness, the happiness, the relaxation – that sense of ease which is peculiar to the seaside in summer, and is evident in everything from the flutter of windbreaks to the sound of children's voices – switched instantly to a sense of fear and panic. The change affected the holiday-makers in different ways: some were immediately on their feet, while others appeared frozen by the suddenness of it all. Of all of them Lynn Hooper was first into the water, moving with a nearly forgotten speed as she passed the instructor. His shouted warnings went unheard or unheeded, his words vanishing into the wall of noise that came from behind him. He even wondered, both then and many times afterwards, if she had known he and her young son were there.

Grace was lucky. The two surfers with her when it happened were Royal Marines making the most of their otherwise unexciting posting at the nearby base. Using their boards as floats, and with Grace held firmly between them, they made it in before the second wave came. Standing dripping on the sand, still unsure of what was happening, Grace looked up the beach. Among the confusion she picked out her father on the tide line, looking out across the reef. Behind him, some way back, she made out the little figure of her brother with their instructor. With her heart gradually slowing, she began to look about for her mother. She was nowhere to be seen. Her eyes tracked back down the beach just in time to see her father start to wade into the water – and it was then that she realised her mother must already be out there.

2

Grace lay on the bed, surrounded by her clothes. When she'd opened the drawers she had found dead flies and drawing pins. The drawing pins had confused her, but it was the dead flies – dozens of them, lying on their backs with their legs arched together in some final prayer – that troubled her. Why, she wondered, had they climbed in there in the first place?

In the past someone had lined each drawer with wallpaper, the pieces cut roughly to shape and curling at the edges. She tried to scoop up the little black bodies with them, but they were so light that they slid off at the slightest movement. Once, she exhaled from the concentration, and several more took flight on her breath. She clamped her lips shut, partly to stop it happening again but partly too to stop them somehow finding their way up and into her mouth when she breathed in. Despite her efforts they were soon scattered on the floor as well as in the drawers. Some fell onto her bare foot, making her jump and flinch at the same time as they worked their way between her toes. She reached down and frantically brushed them off, hopping on her other foot, under which she then felt more crisp bodies. Billy, who had been lying on his own bed and facing the wall, turned to see what was happening. When he began to laugh, the hard bud of desperation in Grace's throat blossomed, and the tightness slackened into tears. Billy was silent again. He turned back towards the wall. A short while later, when her own tears had cleared and she was done sniffing the last of them away, she heard his muffled sobs.

'Hey,' she said, going over and sitting on his bed. She put a hand on his shoulder, and tried to pull him towards her so that she could see his face. He scrunched himself tighter in against the wall. She could see the tears running down over his nose. She stayed as she was, her hand resting on his shoulder. Minutes passed while she tried to think of something to say. Eventually it was Billy who spoke, but his face was pushed so hard against the bed that she couldn't make out a word of it.

'I can't hear you. Come on, sit up and talk to me.' He didn't move. 'Okay, I'll come down. Budge up.' She lay down next to him on the single bed, and put an arm around him. She had meant it as a comfort to him, but now she was there she found that the comfort was hers. He was warm and his clothes still smelt of home. Silently she vowed to hug her brother more.

'You know, I think you might have just set a new world record for someone going from laughing to crying. What was it? About three seconds?' He was breathing a bit easier and she could feel that his body had relaxed now that she wasn't leaning over him. She risked punching him lightly in the ribs. 'Wow, you're good. I've never seen anyone as quick as that before. Definitely a new world record. I'll have to write and tell them. My brother Billy, the fastest laugher-crier in the world, one second he's laughing, the next—'

'Stop …'

'What? You don't want me to write to them?'

Billy struggled free of her arm and wriggled round to face her. The whites of his eyes were tinged with red. She saw the seriousness in his face, a seriousness which came partly from his naturally doleful expression and partly from within, and which made it all the more rewarding to make him laugh – though that was never actually as hard to do as it first seemed. For people who didn't know him well, though, it felt like a triumph to make such a sincere face smile. But at those times when he had done something wrong, which was alarmingly often if his teachers at Maddox Junior School (an institution that proudly announced its 'Special Status' on all official correspondence) were to be believed, that same look of sincerity was often interpreted as one of intent, and simple overexcitement was ruled out as an explanation for his behaviour.

He sniffed and made to speak, but then didn't seem able to find the right words. Grace put her hand on his arm and waited, knowing it would come. He sniffed again.

'I'm sorry I laughed.'

'That's all right. You're an idiot, but that's all right.'

'I didn't mean to make you cry.'

'I wasn't crying because of you. It was all those horrible flies. They were getting everywhere.' She stopped. She could still feel the emotion at her throat, and she swallowed it down. 'It wasn't you, I promise.'

Outside, the sun had moved round, and the room wasn't as brightly lit. Billy said nothing, and when Grace saw the look of bewilderment in his eyes her own unhappiness retreated a little. She wondered how much of any of this he understood.

'Is that why you were crying? Because you thought you'd upset me?'

He looked away, and then nodded.

'Oh, Billy.' She squeezed his arm.

'It's just,' he looked back at her, 'it's just that everyone keeps crying, all the time, even the old people who I didn't think *ever* cried, and it makes me feel strange. Except you. Out of everybody you're the one who's still a bit normal, and then I laugh at you and then you're crying too and I feel even stranger than I did before.' He paused for breath. 'I just wish it would all stop. It makes everyone look so sad and horrible.' His expression changed as he yawned. It passed; his face straightened. 'And it makes me tired too.'

'All right,' said Grace, 'let's make a deal. No more crying. Okay?'

He looked solemnly at her. 'Okay. No more crying. Not unless you have to because you've hurt yourself or something.'

Grace smiled, and then wrapped her serious little brother in a hug.

The rumble of hooves reached the old man in the darkness. He felt it through the ground as much as heard it, and it came from all around. The herd must have split up; they would be panicking. He stopped and stood where he was, breathing hard. On all sides he was surrounded by maize taller than himself, so that he could see no further than the plants immediately in front of him. His trousers were soaked through, the material slick against his skin.

The torch was beginning to dim and he turned it off. The upper tendrils of the crop feathered the edge of the darkness, a decorative hem between land and sky. Only now, with the torch off, did he see the trace of light in the east. In another few hours it would be dawn.

The evening passed slowly. As the light outside began to fade, so Billy grew hungrier. He thought about going downstairs to see if he could find something to eat. But he didn't know where the kitchen was, and he didn't know what he would say to the old man if he was found looking through the cupboards. And anyway, he couldn't move: Grace had fallen asleep on him.

The old man. He thought he recognised him but he wondered if this was only because he thought he ought to, because he'd been told that they had met before. Perhaps if I put him next to five other old men then I wouldn't recognise him, he thought. Perhaps then I'd choose an old man who I'd never even seen before. He tried to think of what he had looked like when they arrived. He had white hair and massive fingers, but that was all he could remember. When he tried to picture it, his face was a blank, wrinkly space. What if right now he was at school, and the old man had come to collect him? And what if other old men had come to collect some of the other children? Would he try to go home with the wrong one, even though he had already seen him earlier that day? He hoped not.

He took a deep breath; his sister's left arm rose and fell with it. Perhaps the tiredness was affecting his imagination. He decided to check, and he closed his eyes and tried to picture some baked beans on toast. Instantly there they were, the steam coming off them. He was so hungry it almost hurt. And just when he thought he could smell them, and nearly taste them, he was asleep.

*

The sound of hooves came again, closer this time. The old man pressed on towards it, pushing himself through the maize. It was late in the season and the stems were thick, the cobs heavy, and between them they made progress slow and difficult. Soon he came upon a corridor that had been smashed through the crop. He flicked the torch back on briefly and studied the ground. The soil was soft and the hoof marks were easy to pick out. To his relief they were headed north, back towards the water-meadows where they had come from. He wondered why they had broken the fence in the first place – there was still plenty of grass on there. No matter. If they found their way back there, to where they could see each other and the things around them, they would begin to calm.

He followed the track made by the animals. He wondered at their power, at the way they had ploughed straight through plants that were strong enough in the stem to force him to struggle between them. Occasionally one of the shattered stalks shifted as he approached it, catching his eye even in the darkness as it adjusted to its new and broken form.

Then came the noise. It was the sound of maize breaking up ahead. He stood perfectly still, feeling the thud of hooves through his feet. He readied himself, willing his eyes to see more than they could. The first cow passed a few yards to his left, boring out a fresh corridor through the crop. It seemed unaware of his presence. The second animal broke cover immediately in front of him, running parallel to the first. Its black and white head and flanks were surprisingly visible in the half-light as it careered towards him. He raised his arms in the air, like some startled night bird about to take flight. 'Go on!' he shouted as he waved up and down. 'Go on! Get on!'

At the last moment the cow veered off. But it wasn't enough to turn them. More of the herd flashed past, the ones closest to him clearly white at the mouth from the exertion. For a short time the night air was thick with the smell of them, a low pungent scent that stirred memories in the old man of the barn that housed them in winter. And then they were gone. They were headed downhill, towards the wire at the south end of the field. In the darkness they would never see it, and beyond the wire was the road.

The old man woke and felt the sweat at his eyes.

It was night when Grace woke. She wondered briefly where she was, but when she realised she was still dressed she knew. One of her arms had lost all its feeling. She moved it carefully so as not to disturb her brother. In the darkness his breathing was slow and even.

She moved across to her own bed and found it was still covered in the clothes from her case. Undressing quietly she climbed in beneath them. She felt empty, and she wondered why their grandfather hadn't called them down for something to eat. Then the memory of the dead flies came back to her. She pictured them lying on the floor just a few feet away, their legs still clasped together. For a time she couldn't sleep for thinking about them, about why so many of them were there in the drawers and why they had died.

She woke again later in the night. From his breathing she knew Billy was awake too, but she didn't say anything, and nor did he. A chill had come in at the window, and she pulled the blanket tighter about herself and listened. Downstairs someone was moving around.

3

Like an abandoned cub, Billy sought out the shade of an open-ended barn that stood opposite the house. By the time he had crossed the farmyard his trainers were covered in dust, the fine particles muting their whiteness. The shade was a relief, but if anything the air inside was even closer.

Unfamiliar smells enveloped him. He stood still for a while, wondering why he had been sent outside. He understood that sometimes adults wanted to be left by themselves, but his sister wasn't an adult. She was only four years older than him. The familiar feeling that he might have done something wrong tugged at him, but all he had done so far today was get up, come down those steep stairs, and eat some breakfast. They'd found some stale bread on the kitchen table, and some funny-tasting butter. There was honey too. It was when he'd asked her where the television was that she'd sent him out here. What was wrong with wanting to watch TV? He screwed up his eyes until they started to hurt, and then opened them again. He decided not to think about it.

To begin with he walked in such a way that suggested he was worried about stepping in something. But after a while he started deliberately kicking up clouds of dust. Soon bits of straw were stuck in his laces, and he had to pull the neck of his T-shirt up to cover his nose. Old bits of machinery lay here and there, half submerged in their own dust, their makers' names faintly visible: John Deere, Deutz Fahr, Massey Ferguson. He tried saying them aloud, to see what they sounded like, but the only one he could really manage was John Deere. His head cocked to one side as he looked at the second word where it was written down in front of him. That was an animal, he knew that, but he thought it was spelt differently. He wasn't sure, but he thought there might be too many 'e's. Certainly there were a lot of them.

He looked at it a while longer, but then both the words started to look strange, so he stopped. That was always happening. If you looked at any word for long enough it stopped making any sense. That's why there was no point even trying to spell things right: if you don't know it, the harder you try the worse it gets. The trick was to just know, and then you didn't get confused. He'd tried telling Miss Avery this before, but he could never make her understand.

It was then that he noticed the green and yellow motif for

the first time. It was a picture of a deer, jumping or about to jump, and Billy basked in the sudden pleasure of being proved right: it didn't have too many 'e's after all. What he'd thought was spelt wrong was spelt right, which proved *he* was right – why did no one ever believe him? Something sprouted from the animal's head, and after a moment's thought he remembered what they were called. *Antlers.* He ran his finger over them, feeling the smoothness of the plastic against the corroding metal. He said the name aloud again, and as he did a cartoon came alive in his head, of a deer called John who walked around on his back legs. He was fat, and had a deep voice and a big mouth that wobbled when he spoke. Billy carried on trailing his finger over the lettering as he imagined him, until all of a sudden it peeled and came away under his touch. He'd broken it: all that was left was the shadow of where it had been. The image in his head of John Deere quickly faded too. He straightened up and glanced over his shoulder. But there was no one there to see him.

He pressed on. Dust hung in the air behind him. High above in the rafters, where the air was at its hottest, dozens of pairs of eyes watched his every move.

Grace hesitated, unsure of what to do. She and Billy had slept late, and when they'd ventured downstairs there had been no sign of the old man. The ground floor of the house was separated by the staircase: to one side the floor was covered by the rug she was on now, and to the other the flagstones had been left bare. The front door was directly opposite the stairs, and several pairs of boots and other shoes stood just inside it, beside a long-handled broom with bristles clogged with dirt. Following a hunch Grace had turned right, and a few short paces later she'd led her brother onto some patterned lino. Cupboards lined the walls, and a stove the colour of redcurrants warmed the room. Standing in the centre was a large wooden table flanked by chairs. The table-top was warped, so that its edges were naturally raised as if it had been specially designed to keep anything from rolling off. When she looked closer she saw that large cracks had opened up along its length, and within these cracks lay a loose mortar of crumbs and other bits of food.

On the table they'd found some stale bread, some butter that smelt like cheese and a jar of honey with a handwritten label. The ink had run, the black stretching into blue. They sat and ate in silence, their hunger outweighing the strange sensation of eating someone else's food in someone else's kitchen, and without that someone else being there. As had been the case for several days now, there had seemed little to say. Eventually it was Billy who spoke. 'I want to watch TV,' he said. 'Not now,' said Grace quietly, as if she thought someone was listening. 'Eat some more bread.' She'd pushed the plate closer to him. 'But I want to watch TV,' said Billy.

Afterwards Grace felt a pang of guilt at sending him outside, but she'd wanted to look around the house alone and she couldn't be sure of what she might find. Once Billy had gone she'd followed the corridor back past the stairs, walking on the rug that had worn through in places, its criss-cross construction exposed where the strands were coming adrift. And now here she was, facing a door that stood slightly ajar.

She pushed it open and stepped inside. Instantly she was cloaked by a stale stillness. A large window took up most of one wall, but because it faced west and it was still the middle of the day, the room was free from any natural warmth. An old-fashioned radio stood on the window-sill, and in a chair in the corner, within an arm's length, sat the old man. He was asleep, his chest rising and falling with asthmatic unease. The terrier was on his lap, curled up against his considerable stomach. Grace watched as its nose twitched, smelling her in its sleep. It woke, blinking sleepily, and she saw the exact moment when it registered her presence. It raised its head, fully awake now, and watched her. One of its ears was torn and broken, and it hung at half-mast beside the undamaged one. It watched her so closely that she wondered if it might be about to growl, but for now at least it remained quiet.

She looked at the old man. His arms were stretched out along both arms of the chair, his fingers curled over the edges as if in a precaution against falling out. The shirt he wore was short-sleeved, and his forearms were thick, each as heavy-looking as a log. The watch on his right arm was so tight that it cut into his wrist. Dense hair struggled out from beneath it. Lines of dirt were ingrained along his fingers, and

31

one of his thumbnails had turned black. As she looked, his fingers tightened around the chair, and those great arms flexed.

For a time she wondered if the chair might break. Each time the old man's grip tightened on it she heard the wood creak. Then the room fell silent, until his arms relaxed again and the wood sighed its relief. It was during the silences that she half expected something to give. Throughout this struggle the dog watched her from his lap, either too used to what was happening to take any notice, or too interested in her to pay it any attention. Under its scrutiny she felt aware of being a stranger in this house, and, at least as far as this room was concerned, an intruder too. She looked through the window at the garden, at the pale uncut grass. She wished she was out there with Billy, wherever he might be. Vaguely remembering something about farms being dangerous, she hoped he hadn't gone far.

'How were those beds?'

Startled, she saw the old man was watching her. He had on some silver-framed glasses that she hadn't noticed before, but which must have been on the table beside him. He had one hand on the dog, his fingers moving almost imperceptibly as he scratched its back.

'Okay,' she said, nodding through her surprise. 'Quite comfy actually.'

The old man raised his eyebrows. 'That's good to hear,' he said. The words rumbled out of him, sections of them half swallowed. 'Only they've not seen a body for a while, and I wasn't sure how much life was left in them.' It's his accent, she realised as he tried to look past her, that's why he sounds like that. 'Your brother with you?'

She shook her head. 'Outside. I should probably go and find him. He has a habit of . . .' She checked herself, not wanting to give the wrong impression. 'Well,' she said, looking outside again, 'I should probably go and look for him. He's only nine, and I know how dangerous farms can be.'

The old man nodded slowly. 'Probably best.' He looked through the window and then back at Grace. He took a breath. 'Probably best,' he said again. He looked up at the patch of sky that was visible. 'The day's getting away from us. It'll soon be dinnertime. Come on, boy. Up.' The dog jumped down, and the chair creaked again as the old man placed both hands on it and raised himself. The dog came over and sniffed at Grace's shoes.

'That's Jackson, by the way. I don't know how you are with dogs, but he won't bother you.' He took another deep breath and fixed her again with his eyes. 'Now then. The two of you must be half starved. You never ate last night.'

'We had some bread and honey. We didn't know where you were, so we helped ourselves.'

He was still looking hard at her and, although she found it unnerving, there was so much to see in his face that she didn't look away. Deep creases in his skin travelled up and down and from left to right, each one petering out as it ran into the next. His nose was big and bulbous, and his ears were like thick onion rings, with a growth of hair sprouting from their centres. His mouth seemed very small, even when he opened it to speak, and she wondered if this too was responsible for his muffled speech.

Finally he nodded. 'You'll need to do that if you're after surviving for very long.' He winced as he straightened up fully. He seemed shorter, and Grace saw that he wasn't wearing any shoes. 'That's fifteen miles to a shop, and I'm not one for going if I don't need to. Especially in this heat.'

They left the room and started back along the passageway, Jackson leading the way. Despite the heat the old man's socks were thick, and he rolled from side to side as he walked, giving the impression that from the waist up his body was too heavy for his legs. Fifteen miles, thought Grace. For the first time she wondered where exactly they were. She tried to remember any signposts from their journey but found she couldn't; she must have forgotten the unfamiliar names almost as quickly as she'd read them. She thought of the hours it had taken to get here, and how she'd texted her friends until her phone had run out of battery. She pictured it lying upstairs next to her bed, fully charged now but still without any signal. It didn't know where it was either.

'So where do you get everything if you don't go to the shops?'

'There's plenty of things that don't want buying,' said the

old man without looking round at her. 'Plenty you can eat, and plenty you can make.'

'I know, I mean I—' started Grace, tripping over her words in her haste to agree. 'That's what I was always trying to tell—' She stopped short, unable to say their names in front of him. She thought he'd turn and look at her, to see what she was talking about, but he didn't. She wasn't even sure he'd heard her.

Jackson's claws clack-clacked on the lino as they arrived in the kitchen. She watched the old man bring out the bread and butter and put them on the curved tabletop. There was something strange about seeing such powerful arms being used to lift small, domestic things. He stopped what he was doing and returned her look.

'You want to eat?'

'No,' she said, unsure if it was a question or an accusation. 'No, thank you.'

He continued to look at her, peering first through and then beneath his glasses, his head tilted back.

'You know, I can see her in you,' he said. 'She's in the boy more, but I can see her in you too. There's no mistaking it.' Not knowing what else to do, Grace just stood there. 'I'm too old for you to see it now,' he went on, 'but not all that long ago she was in me as well.' He pointed at his eyes with the first and second fingers of one hand. 'Right here, clear as day, you couldn't miss it. People used to say as much when they saw us together.'

Still Grace was silent. The more the old man said the fewer words she seemed able to find for herself.

'What I mean to say,' said the old man, pushing his glasses up his nose, 'if I'm not being clear, is that you're both welcome here. Truth is, whether you knew it or not, you always were.'

Back out in the sunlight the smell was almost overpowering. It was as if all the different smells in the barn had been building up to this, and again Billy pulled his T-shirt up over his nose. He looked about for its source, squinting in the glare as his eyes adjusted.

Mostly all he saw were nettles. Lots of them, stacked a hundred deep and buzzing with flies. A butterfly fluttered and landed. It folded its wings and then slowly opened them again, displaying the deep ruby uppers with imitation eyes. He stepped closer for a better look, but the moment he did it took off and danced its way further out of reach. He followed as best he could along the track that ran alongside the nettles, his movements suddenly purposeful. Every time the butterfly flew lower and looked as if it might land again, he rushed towards it in readiness. He wanted to be ready.

But still it didn't land. He rushed on ever faster, deciding now that he would overtake it instead. Its irregular way of flying started to annoy him – it seemed so aimless, so unaware of what he wanted it to do – and such was his hurry and his growing impatience that he didn't see the large flint on the track ahead of him. He pitched face first into the greenery, flinging out his hands to break his fall. Instantly he felt something like electric shocks shooting through them, and he clasped his hands together between his legs, trying to squeeze the pain from them. When that didn't work he held them up before his face, to check to see if they really were on fire. Through his tears he could see the skin already rising into a collection of white dots. He brought them to his mouth and sucked: maybe if he sucked hard enough the pain would stop, like they did in films when a snake had bitten someone. Soon his palms were covered in red blotches from his sucking, and he could feel the grit between his teeth.

He picked himself up. There, just a few feet away, was the butterfly, still bobbing along haphazardly. Bending down he picked up a handful of stones and flung them at it. He bent down again and threw another handful, and then another, the stones making the nettles nod where they landed. The butterfly changed course, tacking back and across and over the track below him. Another volley of stones followed it, and when this last handful landed (and just as he was beginning to take pleasure in attacking the nettles as much as anything) something happened that rooted him to the spot. From out of them, moving with sharp, quick movements, came a rat. It scuttled down the track away from him.

Momentarily, he paused. He'd never seen a rat before. The nearest thing he could compare it to was Herbert, the gerbil at Maddox Primary. They'd found him dead in his cage one morning; Miss Avery had cried and Mr Armstrong had buried him in the flowerbed inside the school gates. But this thing was different. Butterfly and nettle stings forgotten, and the tears already drying on his cheeks, he ran after it.

He'd never been much of a runner. Over the years his enthusiasm for sport in general had been replaced by a learnt wariness. What he seemed good at when he practised alone, like football, was soon shown up when he was in the company of others. In his eyes, the trouble was that the others were almost always better than him, which made him look worse than he really was. A lot of the time, including his recent attempt to surf, he felt that it was his body's fault. It simply didn't do what he wanted it to. But once you had a reputation for not being very good at something, that was it: you were just not very good. There was no way back. It was the same when people thought you did bad things on purpose. As his mother always said, they stopped giving you the benefit of the doubt. He'd always hated that. It was a stupid-sounding thing to give people anyway.

The rat was up ahead. It weaved back and forth, periodically vanishing into the nettles or the grassy strip that ran down the middle of the track. But each time he thought he'd lost it, it reappeared, shuffling rapidly on and then pausing; a staccato movement that was easy to spot. They rounded a bend, and what Billy saw made him stop and stare. Encircled by barbed wire was a round pit the size of a small swimming pool. In its bottom was some sort of murky liquid. It stank. A sign nailed to one of the posts that held up the wire read DANGER: DEEP WATER. But it wasn't the water or its depth that interested him. It was the dozen or so rats that he could see moving around the edges.

The farmyard hadn't seemed very big when they arrived, but since leaving the farmhouse Grace had discovered that around every corner was another building, or a further piece of open ground. She had always imagined farms to be straightforward places, where everything had its purpose, where simplicity ruled. But now she was here, it all seemed a bit haphazard, and she was abruptly aware that finding Billy wasn't going to be as easy as she had expected. Strangest of all were the four metal structures that she had stopped next to, at the top of the yard. At first it had been some wild flowers that had caught her eye, growing among the grass at the base of the structures. She'd bent down and held the pink flower-heads between her fingers, wondering at the precision and delicacy of the petals. How amazing, she thought, to be somewhere where such beautiful things grow naturally around the place. She'd glanced about, and then looked up at the structures that towered over her. Circular in shape and forty or fifty feet tall, they had perfectly conical roofs. Fixed ladders ran up to their very tips. Although clearly not new they were rust-free, and the sun had glinted so strongly on them that she had been forced to shut her eyes.

She stayed like that now, her face tilted towards the sun. The heat on her skin felt good, and she was surprised by the relief she felt at being alone. Out here it was even quieter than it had been in the farmhouse. The silence was soothing, and as she took a deep breath and concentrated on her eyelids, which looked red from within, it was easy to believe that she was back in Greenwich Park, pausing to soak up the sun as she waited for Alice to arrive. Having only to cross the road from her house to be in the park, Grace was almost always there first, but she never minded. She was happy enough to wait near the playground as arranged; often she'd see Mrs Kimsby from a few doors down walking her two chihuahuas, or there'd be someone from one of the sports teams at the university out for a run who knew her mother. If Alice texted to say she was going to be really late, or if it was the weekend and it was likely to be busy, she'd walk up towards the Observatory by herself and find a good spot in the grass. From there she'd enjoy the views over London – she always thought Canary Wharf made it look like some sort of futuristic postcard – and try to spot Alice approaching below. Once she arrived they'd spend the rest of the day sunbathing and people-watching, moving into the shade of one of the plane trees if it became too hot. Occasionally they'd see someone from school, and depending who it was they'd either call them over or keep quiet until they'd passed. Perhaps later they'd walk up and buy some food from one of the mobile vans; there they'd find themselves queuing with tourists, and they'd listen as orders were made with all different kinds of accents. Grace knew she lived somewhere that people came from all over the world to visit, but for her it was simply home, somewhere she had known for as long as she could remember. She knew it was the Observatory that they came to see, but for her that was the least interesting part of the place. For her it was the park itself. She could see it from her room; in the summer she walked through it on her way to school, and during those times when Billy had taken something of hers, or broken it, as was more often the case, the park was always there to escape to, a place where nine-year-old boys were forbidden to roam alone.

The thought of Billy ended the daydream. Reluctant to let it go, but knowing she must, she opened her eyes. The sun reflecting off the metal structures made her squint again, and to change the angle she began to walk around the side of one of them. She ran her hand over the metal, feeling the sun's warmth on it. She rapped on the side and a hollow echo answered her. She rapped harder and the reply came back louder. The rungs of the ladder, when she came to it, were worn smooth. She reached out to touch one, but as her hand approached it there was a sudden bang on the metal, making her jump. The echo hung in the air.

She stayed as she was, unsure. Then, carefully, she walked on around to where she'd been moments earlier. Another bang and echo sounded, and she jumped again.

'Billy? Is that you?'

There was no reply, and she carried on walking, quickening her pace. Two more bangs sounded. Picturing her brother hiding on the other side, she turned and ran as fast as she could back around in the opposite direction, keeping her footfalls as quiet as possible. She was still gaining speed, and beginning to feel a touch childish, when she ran headlong into someone who wasn't Billy.

The old man paused for breath before taking another bite. Through the window he saw the heat, but behind the stone walls of the kitchen he felt none of it. Besides the heat there was the girl, and he had watched as she hurried off to find her brother.

It wasn't true, what he'd said. She was so like Lynn he'd nearly believed it was her standing before him. Watching her, he'd seen that even her long-legged, loping way of walking was the same. For a moment it was enough to make him believe that Margaret was still alive, that when he turned back around he would find her sitting at the kitchen table.

But of course she wasn't. He felt a trace of disappointment ebb from him as he buttered another piece of bread. He reached down and gave it to Jackson. The terrier swallowed it whole, then resumed watching his master with bright-eyed eagerness.

The old man got up and stood still on the lino for what to anyone watching would have seemed like a long time.

Then, with crumbs still at the corners of his mouth, he walked to the door opposite the stairs and opened it. Jackson trotted out into the thirsty-looking grass, reappearing a minute or two later.

Looking out into the brightness, he wondered if a place could come to know a person the way a person could know a place. Was it possible that the farm too would see the similarities in them, would sense that they belonged to the same family that had lived and worked here for so many lifetimes? He reached down and scratched Jackson behind the ear. He shook his head, knowing the idea was fanciful. But even then the thought lingered, and he was content to let it.

He felt something stirring deep within him. It was so sudden and unfamiliar that he stayed exactly as he was, bent over like that, not daring to move as he tried to identify it. At first he found only the same sadness as before, but then he found something else, nearly hidden among it and unseen until now. For a time he didn't recognise it – or perhaps instead it was that the habit of grief wouldn't allow him to – but then he knew that what he was experiencing was hope. With the arrival of the girl and the boy, with the echoes of their mother that their faces carried, he felt as if something had been returned to him.

Grace brushed grit from her hands. The larger bits left indentations in her palms. Straightening up she stared at the man before her. She thought it was a man, anyway. He was wiry,

43

not much taller than her, and had tightly curled hair. He was also covered in dust. He looked as if he'd had all the moisture wrung out of him, and been left out in the sun to dry.

'What were you doing?' she said, quick to cover her embarrassment. 'Banging like that?'

The man smiled at her, which made him look younger. His eyes were set close together, the bridge of his nose barely squeezing between them. He really is covered in dust, thought Grace, looking him up and down. She pushed her hair back and waited for him to say something. He was still smiling, and when she kept her eyes on him he started shifting from one foot to the other. The sharp smell of sweat reached her.

'Someone come knocking so I knocked back,' he said abruptly, 'knocking on the bin, I mean, knocking bang bang like this.' He thumped the metal and the echo sounded. He hit it again, much harder this time, and the echo lingered for longer. He looked back at her expectantly.

The noise faded, and Grace saw that his explanation, such as it was, was over. It was her turn.

'I thought you were my brother.' Saying it made her worry again. Billy's knack for being wherever he shouldn't be was unparalleled; their mother had used to say it was his special gift. 'If there's a well to fall down, your brother will find it.' And so it had always been, this the essential difference between them. Through some accident of nature she could look after herself, while her brother required all the help he could get. Now it was down to her to provide that help. Her and the old man, her and their grandfather. She pushed the thought from her mind.

The dusty man was shaking his head. 'No, not your brother, not got a brother. Not got a sister neither.'

'Well, what have you got?'

He chewed his tongue for a while as he thought. His face brightened.

'Layers,' he said, pointing over his shoulder towards a wire enclosure that she hadn't noticed. 'I got layers. And eggs.' She must have looked confused because then he said, 'Egg layers, feathers and feet.' He thought for a moment, as though trying to find another way to make her understand, but in the end he simply said it again, 'Eggs.' He glanced hopefully at her.

'Chickens!' she said, seeing the various shapes moving about behind the wire. 'You've got chickens!'

Without warning he smacked the metal again, making her flinch. This time the echo boomed back at them. He'd hit it so hard that she looked to see if there was a dent, or if he'd hurt his hand. But the metal was undamaged, and he grinned at her. She smiled faintly back.

'Do you think maybe you could stop doing that? The hitting, I mean. What *are* these things, anyway?'

'Bins,' said the man. 'Bins, bins for grain.' Cat-quick he took her by the hand and led her around to the back of the four structures. He pointed out over a field of barley. 'Grain in the field then grain in the bins.' He pointed at the metal. 'I throw grain for the layers, then eggs.' He gave her another of his smiles that made him look younger. 'Then breakfast.'

She smiled, reassured by the simplicity of his description. So these buildings did make sense after all. She looked out over the field. They really were on a proper farm, where grain was grown only yards away from the chickens that ate it. She was so pleased that the words automatically started grouping themselves into sentences, sentences that would rush from her mouth as she told her parents. As if convincing them to grow their own vegetables hadn't taken long enough, for over a year now she'd been trying to persuade them to keep chickens.

An iciness spread through her. There would be no more persuading. She caught her breath, feeling the warm sensation in her eyes that she knew was the precursor to tears. The whole idea was too huge, too unfathomable; even though she knew it to be true, she could only understand it for a few seconds at a time.

She looked again at the man. Beads of sweat were clearing paths through the dirt on his forehead.

'Who are you?' she said.

'Spider.'

'That's not a name.'

'Spider. Incy-wincy spider.'

She saw that he meant it. She looked afresh at the small

man in front of her. Those strange eyes that were so close together and so pale. She began to wonder if he was really a man at all: it was as if his body had raced ahead, leaving his mind floundering in childhood. In spite of his smiles she sensed the struggle in him, and even as they stood there she pictured him surrounded by other children in a playground, all of them chanting '*Incy-wincy spider, incy-wincy spider*' at him over and over, until he did the only thing he could and accepted it as his name.

'Spider's a nice name,' she said, immediately hating herself for how it sounded. That was the way people talked to Billy. Usually they were the ones who thought they were good with children too. But the effect of her words was clear; the compliment had found its mark. The man shifted from foot to foot, as if the ground beneath him was painfully hot, and he could no longer meet her eye.

'So how come you're called that?' she asked.

He shifted once more from one foot to the other.

'Watch the Spider,' he said.

Again she was amazed by the speed of him. In an instant he was on the ladder on the side of one of the grain bins. She watched as he virtually ran up it, his arms and legs working in unison to bear him upwards. In no time at all he was at the very top. He waved at her, a small figure framed against the blue of the sky. Then, with equal speed, he climbed back down, dropping off the ladder long before he reached the lower rungs and landing with a thump. He stood before her, puffing only very lightly and clearly pleased with himself.

She shook her head, not knowing what to do except smile. He grinned back at her uncontrollably, and started shifting from one foot to the other even quicker than before. And although it was impossible to tell under all the dust, and that there was a good chance that any colour she thought she might have seen was sunburn, she suspected he was blushing.

'I bet you can see for miles from up there.'

'See for miles,' he repeated, his eyes widening, 'green and yellow like a flying bird. Upside down for you and me.'

The smell of sweat coming off him was stronger now, and when it reached her it brought her to her senses.

'I have to go,' she said. 'I need to find my brother.'

'Best place for finding is up there,' said Spider. He looked up. 'Find anything up there.'

Grace glanced at the ladder. Billy might be inside a barn, it was true, and it was true too that she wasn't a big fan of heights. But the ladder was obviously safe – that at least had just been demonstrated – and if he was out in the open she might spot him immediately.

She walked over and stood by the bottom rung. All the fear seemed to have gone out of her. Is this it? she wondered. Ever since it had happened she'd been waiting to see how she would change; recently she'd begun to worry that she might not change at all, that she might remain the same Grace

Hooper for ever, even after everything. So maybe this *was* it. In a way it made sense: why should she be scared of anything now?

As if to prove it, she began to climb. As she went she became aware of how quiet it was. Even the birds seemed to have stopped singing, and she imagined them collectively holding their breath as they watched her. This girl wanted to be like them. She was taking to the sky.

Billy's arm was beginning to ache. He paused between throws and looked at the pile of stones on the concrete. At least half of them were still left, and there were some good ones too. The big ones were hard work but worth the effort; even if they fell short they made a good splash. The average-sized ones were the best all-rounders for throwing: you could get power *and* accuracy, and because of this there weren't many of these left. Finally there were the small, lightweight ones which, although easier on the arm, were too light to be really effective. Because of the concrete he'd been forced to find his ammunition elsewhere, and then transport it back to the pit using his T-shirt as a carrying sling. As he bent down to reload, he reflected that he probably should have made lots of little trips rather than one big one. His T-shirt, as well as being very dirty, now hung down almost as far as his knees. He felt like he was wearing one of his sister's dresses.

*

The metallic chill of the rungs was reassuring. In her mind Grace fostered the idea of a connection between cold metal and unbreakable strength. But then, as she gained height and the grain bin was afforded less shade by its neighbour, the temperature started to rise. Along with the added heat came a breeze that hadn't been present on the ground, and it seemed to her that she was truly somewhere else.

Looking down she saw Spider directly below her. He'd moved to the bottom of the ladder almost as soon as she'd started to climb, and now he stood with one foot on the first rung, as if ensuring its stability. Or perhaps he's intending to climb up behind me, she thought. But he stayed as he was, watching, and when a few rungs later the breeze worked its way under her clothes and moved over her, she sensed his gaze there with it.

She reached the lip of the bin, where the conical top began. The angle of the ladder eased and she found herself walking almost normally, though not once did she let go of the handrails. The farm slowly came into view below her. The two large, open-ended barns dominated the scene, but smaller, older-looking sheds and buildings cluttered the edges. The oldest of these were close by, and she saw the broken tiles and the moss growing in the gutters. In places the brick walls were stained by the dripping of rainwater. There too was the chicken run, the individual birds easier to see from up here as they scratched about in the dust. Looking the other way, she saw at the centre of the farmyard an open space, a concrete area sectioned off by a network of fencing and gates. All the gates were open.

She tried to trace the way she had come. The white farmhouse with its windows and chimneys was easy to spot. The buildings looked quite different from above, and she saw what Spider meant. In a way it was like seeing everything upside down. Instead of looking up at their walls and ceilings, she was looking down onto their roofs.

A sudden giddiness came over her. She sat down and concentrated on the stitching in her jeans, gulping down breaths while she waited for it to pass. After a while she dared to look again. Far below, the field of barley stretched away before her. Here and there poppies interrupted the uniform yellow in bursts of red, like drops of blood spilt from above. Beyond lay another field, almost identical to the first. Oak trees rose out of the hedge that separated them.

She was about to look away when a flash of light in the far field caught her eye. She looked again, narrowing her eyes to see in the brightness, and there was another flash, and another. They came slowly, and she realised she was watching the blades of wind turbines catch the sun as they made their unhurried circuits in the breeze. They had learnt about wind farms in Mr Beazley's class; before Christmas he'd taken them to see one in the school minibus. It was huge, and Grace remembered seeing that strange word ECOTRICITY written in letters taller than her along its length. They were the future. The oil was running out and when it did these odd-looking things would supply all the electricity they needed. Best of all, no one owned the wind, and it would never run out. *Renewable.* That was the word Mr Beazley always emphasised, his thick moustache wriggling like a caterpillar as he said it over and over, pacing up and down between their desks.

She thought about the last time she was sitting in one of his lessons, surrounded by the rest of her class. How they were all counting down the days until the holidays, swapping plans for those precious weeks of freedom. She remembered the pride she'd felt when she told everyone that they weren't going abroad this year; she remembered too how she'd been sure to say it loud enough for Mr Beazley to hear. 'We're going to Devon to learn to surf,' she'd said. What she didn't tell them about were the weeks of negotiating that had preceded this decision, with Grace holding her father's passport aloft as if it was some kind of magical artefact that would win the argument for her. '*Fourteen* flights in *six* months?' she'd said, as if this was something she had only just discovered, as if her father's regular absence on work trips had always puzzled her up until now. 'How can you justify it? The ice-caps are melting, polar bears are dying, and you think it's all right to fly –' she paused while she double-checked the passport, '– *twelve* times in the last year? And that's only the ones that are marked here.' Having tried for some time now to laugh the whole environment thing off ('Okay, eco-girl, let's move out into the park and make our clothes out of leaves') her father had looked straight at her. 'Grace,' he'd said, 'I'm a travel writer. The clue's in the name. I wouldn't be a very good one if I didn't actually travel.'

Grace had been unimpressed. 'Come on, this stuff is really *happening*, we have to change the way we live or there'll be no—' she looked to the ceiling, exasperated, 'there'll be no *anything*. There'll just be one big sea. There won't be anywhere left to write about.' She glanced back at him and Lynn in turn (they had been Lynn and Michael from the very beginning, never Mum and Dad), awaiting their response. Billy, who up until then had been carefully pulling at a loose thread on the arm of the sofa, and who apparently cared less about all this than anyone, looked up from the ever-lengthening piece of material. 'We could still go swimming,' he said. A smile started to take shape on Michael's face, and he had to look away. 'Yes, I suppose we could,' said Lynn levelly, and then, 'Oh Billy, darling, please don't do that; the whole thing'll fall apart if you keep pulling at it.' Sensing that her argument was falling away along with their attention, Grace had switched strategy. 'Think how much money we'd save if we stayed here. And – and no airports, no languages we can't speak, and—' 'Where then?' interrupted Michael, his eyes focused back on hers, the truth being that he disliked airports and air travel more than he would ever admit; there too, at the back of his mind, was an inkling that this might be something he could write about. 'Where in

England are we going to spend a week without getting bored, or fed up with being rained on?'

And that was the turning point. She'd gone straight over to the computer and shown them a picture of Briscombe Bay, and the cottage just through the dunes. Afterwards, when it was agreed, she'd carried that same picture around in her head for the remaining weeks of term. Those two rocks in the water, the ones Michael had thought he was being funny in renaming Laurel and Hardy. Those same two rocks that were responsible for the break, and the rip too.

She'd learnt a lot about rips since then. Water became trapped behind the reef, prevented by subsequent waves from escaping back out to sea. That day it was stronger than usual because of the onshore wind and the low tide, and the only way out was through the two channels on either side of the reef. Even now she could remember the strength of it as it took her out. And then, out of nowhere, came the waves. It had made the national news: that evening at the police station a television had been on, and she'd listened as scientists did their best to explain what had happened. Two phrases in particular had stayed with her – 'wave fields' and 'focal zones' – as if the words alone would offer some sort of comfort if she studied them for long enough. There were arguments between lifeguards about the lack of red danger flags; there were interviews with passengers on a ferry that was hit and nearly sunk by similar waves in the Irish Sea a few years ago; there was even the suggestion that freak waves such as these were happening all the time. For Grace, the idea that the waves could have been travelling for hours, perhaps even days, moving silently and harmlessly across the ocean before finally exploding – as if enraged to suddenly find land in their way – into Briscombe Bay, was mesmerising. That it coincided precisely with her and her brother's first surfing lesson was beyond comprehension. She remembered how despite the warning not to fight the water the panic had risen quickly in her, and before she knew what she was doing she was struggling franticly. If it hadn't been for the two Royal Marines it was likely that Billy would be here by himself. This alone made the responsibility she felt for her brother feel heavier still; despite everything, *she had been lucky*. That was what they'd kept saying to her, the police and then the social worker. But each time she heard it she'd known more surely than before that she hadn't been anything of the kind.

She took a breath and tried to clear her mind. But the memory of that day refused to be banished, and once more she was on the beach, running towards where her father had been standing only moments earlier. She hadn't gone far when something heavy hit her from behind; and then, with the rush of water loud in her ears, she was being borne aloft, carried up the beach. She remembered how when one of the soldiers from before finally put her down the sand was hot and dry to the touch; getting to her feet, she saw they were nearly at the dunes. Turning, she looked with disbelief at the scene below her. The whole beach was white with foam. Here and there people staggered through it, clutching at one another for support. Debris lay everywhere, from brightly coloured beach equipment to long, straggly lines of seaweed. For a time it was impossible to tell where the beach ended and the sea began, but as she continued to look the foam soaked away, and the divide became clear once more.

The soldier was gone, running back down the beach to help a woman who seemed unable to stand. Grace tried to work out where it was that she'd seen Michael, and then began to wander in that same direction. It all looked so different. The wailing of children reached her, and she realised the rushing noise was gone. The image of her brother standing with Tim the instructor returned to her, and she glanced about. People were congregating up near the car park, and she could hear voices shouting instructions. She paused, torn between searching up there and on the beach. Had she really seen her father begin to wade into the water? Maybe she'd been mistaken – about Lynn too. Perhaps she'd gone to get an ice cream for Billy? Or jogged back to the cottage for something? But deep down she knew. For whatever reason, she'd been out there already.

She reached the shore. Plastic bags and towels floated in the shallows. Up ahead she saw the figure of a man standing with his hands on his knees, and momentarily her heart skipped with hope. But as she drew nearer she saw that it wasn't Michael. She watched the man scoop sand from his mouth with his fingers; his swimming trunks hung loosely from him, ripped nearly in two, and when he saw her he held them against himself. Seeing him made what had happened seem real; yet as she stood there she also had a sense that she was watching herself from afar. She felt the fear taking shape within her, an ugly thing that began as a tightening in her stomach. Can this really be happening, she asked herself, glancing out again over the water, can I really be standing here alone, wondering if my parents are still out there? Is this possible?

She heard sirens. Up at the car park the police had arrived, and when she looked she saw there were ambulances too. Remembered now, those moments felt like the last in which she'd had any sort of control over her life. A police-woman started speaking through a loud hailer, instructing everyone to leave the beach and return to the car park. On her way there Grace had found herself walking alongside others, and when she saw the shock in their faces she supposed her face might look the same. One woman was crying as she walked, and several times the man beside her had to prevent her from turning back. She kept repeating something through her tears, and it was a while before Grace realised she was saying a name. 'Geor-gi-na,' she said again and again, each syllable separated by a sob, 'Geor-gi-na.' 'Listen to me,' the man had said, his arm around her shoulders, 'right now no one knows where anyone is, so try not to panic, okay?' The man's voice wavered as he spoke, but even so Grace had repeated the words to herself, doing her best to stay calm. But when she reached the assembly of people and saw Tim and Billy standing together, she knew for a second time. And then, like now, perched alone on top of the grain bin, she had begun to cry.

She sniffed, wiping her nose with the back of her hand. Already the last of her tears had dried on her face, leaving the skin tighter than before. She was annoyed with herself; each time she cried it made her feel weaker. She remembered her deal with Billy. But they'd been told that they should cry if they wanted to, that it was 'healthy'. She'd never heard the word healthy used like that before, and she hadn't liked it. It sounded too much like an attempt to make something bad seem good, a way of dressing up the unhappiness she felt. There was nothing good about any of this, and it was pointless pretending otherwise.

She dared to look down, scanning the ground below to see if Spider had seen her crying. But there was no sign of him, and she imagined him still standing at the base of the ladder, awaiting her return. She raised her head and followed the view around. To the east of the farm the land dropped away into green meadows. This time a stream caught the sun, and her eyes lingered; it looked cooler down there. She forced them on, continuing her circular scan of the farm and hoping to spot Billy at any moment. But it was so hot up there: the metal of the bin reflected the sun all around her, and already she felt as if she was burning. She was half aware that her concentration was wandering, her thoughts muddled by the memories of what had happened. Spider had made it look so easy, but she began to wonder at her decision to climb up there herself. Now she was up here she felt dizzy and sad, and looking around at the spread of buildings for Billy only made it worse. The dizziness came again, and she wondered if she might black out and lose her footing, and tumble to her death. She waited, not completely convinced that this would be a bad thing.

It passed. The breeze picked up: it felt fresh on her face. She stood and steadied herself against the handrail. Then, step by step she rewound her movements, descending backwards. She tried to keep her thoughts to a minimum as she went, and instead, something else started to crystallise in her mind. The view of the farmhouse returned to her, along with the image of the old man asleep inside it. The two big barns, the sheds, the old mossy gutters. The fenced-off area of concrete with all the gates left open. The silence. Something was missing. There were the crops in the fields, and there was the strange man called Spider on the ground below her. There were his layers, his chickens. But all these buildings and all this space suggested something else, something that was no longer there.

4

Grace watched from the kitchen table as the old man drew the knife towards himself, the skins curling upwards until all the potatoes sat on the rough block of wood that served as a chopping board, each as anaemic-looking as the last. Opposite her sat Billy. His T-shirt was filthy and stretched beyond belief, the cotton lying crumpled in his lap. Try as she might ('It's our first proper evening here; it'd be nice if you didn't look like you've been living in a ditch for a week'), he'd refused to change. His explanation when she asked him sort of made sense, but in the usual roundabout way all his explanations did. 'Rats,' he'd said, his eyes wide. 'Loads of them, big ones too. I tried getting them with stones but there weren't any, so I had to go and get some and carry them back. And afterwards my shirt had grown. I didn't do it on purpose, if that's what you mean.' He'd paused, before adding quietly, 'It's your fault for sending me outside.' Ordinarily she might have tried harder to understand, or argue, but the mention of rats was enough. She didn't need to hear any more.

They ate in silence. The potatoes were combined with a stew that the old man ladled out of a cast-iron pot. Although she found the food hot and comforting, Grace was surprised to see Billy eating something so unfamiliar to him with such enthusiasm. Traditionally his favourite food was fish fingers; so suspicious was he of anything that didn't come covered in a crispy batter that lately Lynn had taken to deep-frying vegetables just to get them down him. It had worked. Grace remembered the sickly smell of oil that would permeate the whole house afterwards, and how she'd close her bedroom door in an attempt to keep it out. Her bedroom. She put down her spoon and began to picture it. The pictures on the wall above her bed. All her things on the shelves ...

No, she told herself. I mustn't. Under the table she clenched her hands together. To distract herself she described her meeting with Spider to the old man. From somewhere within him she thought she detected a chuckle. 'He's nothing but a hobbityhoy,' he said between mouthfuls. Grace looked blankly at him. 'Neither a man nor a boy,' he explained when he saw her expression. 'He and his mother live a couple of miles away. He's been helping out on the farm since he was younger than you are now. I let him keep his chickens here, and that keeps me in eggs.'

When they were all finished they sat back in their chairs. The old man's creaked as he did so, reminding her of earlier that day when she'd found him asleep. It seemed so long ago now that she found it hard to believe this was only their second night. The thought worried her. Up until now everything had happened quickly, but since their arrival on the farm it was as if time had grown, had stretched and widened into something unrecognisable, like Billy's T-shirt.

Rising to his feet, the old man collected the peelings from the sink. Going over to where a heavy curtain stretched from ceiling to floor, he pulled it to one side. Behind it was a door.

'Now then. There's two others you need to meet, and then that's that all done with.'

From their places at the table Grace and Billy watched as he opened the door and, without waiting for them, went through it.

'I thought it was just him that lived here,' whispered Billy after a few seconds.

Grace nodded. 'Me too.'

As she looked at the door, out of nowhere came a sense of being back at home in Greenwich. This time there was no resisting it. She and Billy were sitting at the kitchen table, eating breakfast. Lynn had just told Billy that she was leaving in five minutes, before going through the door into the sitting room. Grace knew she would be rushing to get to the university; right now, to save time, she'd be getting Billy's things ready for him. A warmth began to spread through Grace. She could almost smell the porridge that her mother made every morning without fail, regardless of the time of year; there too was the cup of coffee that Michael carried about with him at this time of day, the one he seemed happier to hold than to drink. Soon, when Lynn reappeared, he would suggest that perhaps this morning, if she was running late, he take Billy. It was an offer he made regularly, almost automatically it seemed at times to Grace, and one that Lynn rarely even acknowledged. And so he would continue to pad about the kitchen in his slippers, cradling his coffee as he made toast. It was only after Lynn and Billy had gone, and as Grace herself was getting ready to leave, that he would withdraw to his study. When she shouted that she was off too, she would hear the change in him from the tone of his reply: he was at work now. 'He's on his travels,' Lynn used to say when he was writing, and in a sense he really was, for it was in that study that the trips he took were transformed into books and articles.

Billy's chair scuffed loudly against the lino as he stood up. The spell broken, Grace too got to her feet. The warmth she'd been feeling dissipated as she followed him to the door. In its place came the familiar sadness and, as had become her habit, she pushed it to one side.

Outside, in the lee of the house, they found themselves in

63

a small paddock. Thistles grew here and there, their purple crowns reddish and nearly luminous in the evening sun. A rotten-looking fence ran around three sides of the rectangle of grass, and the fourth was provided by the farmhouse itself. An oil tank stood against the wall next to a water trough, and just over the fence was a vegetable patch, immediately identifiable by the neat rows of greenery. The old man was only a few yards away, and when he saw them he turned and looked up the paddock. Following with their eyes they saw two donkeys ambling towards them.

Grace looked at her brother. His usual grave expression was unchanged, but by his sides his hands twitched back and forth as though of their own accord. It was something he had always done when he was excited, and was something she teased him about in her crueller moments.

'Now then,' said the old man as the animals approached, 'the one on the left is the one you need to watch.'

'What do you mean, "watch"?' said Grace.

He looked at her askance, his head tilted to one side. She tried again. 'Why do we need to watch it?' she said, louder and slower this time, aiming her words at the hairy centre of his ear.

His head went back with understanding. 'He's friendly enough. But if he gets the chance he'll bite you. Trouble is he's never grown up – he's not needed to. That other one's his mother. He's still her little man.' He threw the peelings on the ground in front of them.

It had never occurred to Grace that a donkey could bite you. Dogs, yes, and obviously cats could scratch and bite as well, but a donkey? She'd always thought of them as slow, friendly animals that never did anything in particular except stand about in fields and appear in nativity plays. She watched them come closer. They reminded her of the old man: thick around the middle and with legs that looked too thin to support their upper halves. Their hooves were tiny: they were so dainty they almost looked sharp.

'What's their names?' said Billy.

The old man frowned. 'Names? This is a farm, not a pet shop. Everyone knows animals on farms don't have names.' He was silent for a moment, before putting a hand on Billy's shoulder. With his other hand he pointed at the larger of the two donkeys. 'That's Jenny, and her boy's Easter. Born Easter morning, twenty-eight years ago.'

'So how old's *Jenny*?' said Grace.

'Must be getting on for forty. I first got her to break a bull. She's still strong too – you want to sit on her?'

Grace froze, before realising that he didn't mean her. Beside her Billy nodded, and the old man lifted him onto the donkey's back.

The animal still had her nose in the peelings, and she didn't even raise her head as Billy straddled her. He could feel the life beneath him as she ate, and when she shifted her footing he reached forward and held on to her neck. Her coat was soft, more like fur than hair. When the peelings were finished and she raised her head, Billy let go. His hands felt oily. The animal's ears were in front of him now, and he reached forward and scratched them, the same way he'd seen the old man scratch Jackson's a little earlier. It seemed to like it.

Then came the pain. In an instant the old man's hand struck the other donkey's nose, making its head leap up and away from Billy's leg as if it had been stung. Grace too jumped back at the suddenness of it. The donkey turned and arced away from them at a trot.

The older donkey hadn't moved. The old man lifted Billy off her back, and then held him aloft as he examined the bite. Grace could see the tears in her brother's eyes. The leg was already bruising badly, coming up both above and below the bone. Billy flinched as the old man ran a thumb over it.

'He got hold of you all right,' he murmured. 'But the skin's not bust.' He set him down on the grass. 'Can you walk?'

He hobbled a few paces.

'There much pain?'

He nodded. 'It's when I bend it.'

'Mmm?'

'He said it's when he bends it,' said Grace. She watched as the skin continued to colour up. When she looked closer she saw the imprints left from the donkey's teeth. 'It looks horrible.'

'That's nothing but a bit of bruising under the skin,' said the old man. 'It's the muscle that hurts. With a bit of rest he'll be all right soon enough.' He lowered himself stiffly to his haunches in front of Billy. 'Do you think you'll make it?'

Billy looked down at his leg and then back at the old man. He nodded. His face had gone very pale. At the other end of the paddock the donkey that had bitten him stood watching them. It raised its top lip at Grace and bared its teeth. She turned back to the old man.

'I still think he should get it looked at.'

The old man remained as he was. Once again she wondered if he'd heard her, but something about his manner told her that he had. He straightened up. Picking Billy up with one arm he carried him back into the farmhouse, and then on past Jackson who had remained in the safety of the kitchen. Grace followed, shutting the door as she went. She could hear the old man's steps on the stairs, and by the time she caught up with them Billy was lying on his bed, his leg propped up on a pillow. The pose made his T-shirt look like a very dirty hospital gown. 'Keep it up like that,' the old man was saying to him in a low voice, 'it'll throb less. And don't worry yourself about the pain. It'll go soon enough.'

Grace watched from the door, not knowing what to do. She felt sure Billy's leg was bad enough to need a doctor, but she didn't dare say anything more. Something else persuaded her to keep quiet too. She couldn't help feeling that by showing her and Billy the little hidden paddock and the donkeys, he had – in his own way – been welcoming them.

*

Grace sat on the edge of Billy's bed, listening for any sign of the old man's return. None came. She looked down at Billy, and was relieved to see some of the colour returning to his cheeks.

'Does it hurt a lot?'

Billy shook his head, perhaps a little too vigorously, she thought.

'Not if I'm still. It's like the pain's waiting in the air all around my leg, but if I don't move it doesn't know to hurt me.'

Grace leant forward and looked at the rag the old man had tied around her brother's leg. It was soaked in vinegar, and already some of the liquid had leaked onto the sheet.

'Let's get rid of this horrible thing anyway. It's making you smell like a chip shop.' She reached over towards the knot, thinking that perhaps for now she could hang it outside their window.

'I want to keep it on.'

'Why?'

'He said it'd help it to hurt less.'

'But Billy, it's just vinegar. What can vinegar do?'

'I don't care. I want to keep it on.'

Looking at him, she saw that he meant it. Not knowing what else to say, she moved over to her own bed and got in. She lay there thinking, while outside it gradually grew darker. She hoped she might start feeling sleepy before her thoughts returned to the accident. But then there it was: once again she was back on the beach. Knowing the only thing to do was to let it run itself out, she allowed the memory to unfurl.

She remembered how, for a time at least, it had looked as if everything was going to be okay. It seemed a separate group of people had gathered at the far end of the beach, and when they heard the loud hailer they too had made their way to the car park. Now, all around her, people were hugging each other and crying with relief. For a second she imagined herself as one of them, her eyes flitting from face to face as she searched the group for Lynn and Michael.

Standing between her and Billy, their instructor Tim said nothing. Only later, when the police asked anyone who needed to report someone missing to come forward, did he make any move at all. Grace and Billy followed in silence. When Grace glanced at her brother, she saw his expression was unchange, his attention focused on the ambulances and police cars.

'Mr and Mrs Hooper,' she heard Tim say to the policeman. 'Michael and Lynn,' she'd added quickly, feeling a sudden importance was attached to their names. The officer looked at her and Billy, and then back at Tim. 'And you are?' 'Their surf instructor. I was mid-lesson when it happened.' The officer paused as he wrote something down. And then came perhaps the worst part of all: the officer asked Tim to describe what had happened, and she could only stand there and listen.

He told how Lynn had run past him, as if she hadn't seen that he was already carrying her young son up the beach. He told how he'd tried to warn her, but how she'd gone into the water anyway. When the policeman asked why he thought she might have left the safety of the beach, he thought for a while and then said something that Grace had known she would remember for ever. 'I can only think she went in after the girl.' She'd watched as the officer made a note of this too.

She heard a woman crying. When she looked over she saw it was the woman she'd been walking beside on her way back from the beach. The same man had his arm around her, and was doing his best to prevent her from seeing the body of a small girl as it was carried past her. Grace's shock at seeing the limp body, and knowing with such certainty that she was dead, was heightened by the realisation that she knew her name: Georgina. And then it occurred to her that her name was useless now: she wasn't looking at a person called Georgina, but at a dead body. She thought of Lynn and Michael, and the importance she had attached to their names only minutes before.

Everything speeded up after that. There seemed to be more police than before, and the sound of a helicopter came from overhead. She and Billy were shepherded away from the woman and her dead child, and they soon found them- selves in the back of a police car. Grace could remember the heat and the smell of neoprene from their drying wetsuits, as well as the excited way that Billy looked around. As they drove away she saw Tim watching them through the window. It was the last she would see of him.

The first place they stopped was the cottage. To begin with Billy refused to get out of the car, and it was only when Grace promised him that they would be coming back that he conceded. While they changed out of their wetsuits the two police officers searched the other rooms. She remembered hearing voices through the open window, and for a second her heart leapt. But when she looked it was only the same two officers, chatting as they waited by the car, their hats off in the heat. Turning back to the room, she saw the wetsuit Michael had bought her lying on her bed. There was an ordinariness about the way it lay there, exactly as she'd left it that morning. She remembered wishing it was then and not now.

They were watching television at the police station when Billy announced he was hungry. She bought him a bag of crisps and some chocolate from a vending machine, and then watched him eat with a mixture of sadness and admiration. The television was showing pictures of the Empire State Building glowing purple and gold, in honour of the Queen's Golden Jubilee. The picture cut to a long-haired man playing a guitar on the roof of Buckingham Palace, and then the words BREAKING NEWS flashed up on the screen. Instantly Grace's stomach felt as if it had set into something hard. According to the news there had only been one fatality at Briscombe; three others were still missing, and she realised that Lynn and Michael were two of those three. She found herself wondering who the third was.

The experts were still discussing the possible causes of the waves when a large, red-haired woman walked in. 'Oh, for pity's sake,' she said when she saw Grace and Billy, before going straight over to the television and switching it off at the plug. She wore so many necklaces that she jangled when she walked; Grace could remember thinking, as she turned back towards them, that her lipstick contrasted too strongly with her hair. Almost immediately there had been something about her that she hadn't liked, even before she started making decisions for them. 'My name's Elizabeth, but you can call me Liz,' she'd said as she sat down, smiling at each of them in turn. She was slightly out of breath and there were traces of lipstick on her teeth. Grace noticed the sweat on her top lip. 'I'm here to make sure you're looked after properly until we know what's what. That okay with you two?'

Grace had said nothing. She wished she could turn the television back on; she thought to call Alice too, but neither seemed possible with this woman there. 'Are you a teacher?' Billy had asked her. 'No dear,' she'd replied. 'As I said, I'm here to make sure you're cared for.' And then Grace had realised: she was nothing to do with the police – she was a social worker.

Lying in the vinegary gloom, her eyelids began to droop.

She let them go, grateful for the release that was finally being offered by sleep.

That night the dew fell heavily, coating the fields like a thin rain. Mist came down with it, and the first light of day showed the farm swathed in a blanket of white. The four aluminium grain bins rose out of the mist; along the hedges oak trees marked out the farm tracks that were hidden beneath them. In the milking parlour the woodpigeon knew nothing but the stirring of her two chicks, while downstairs in the farmhouse the old man dreamt of strangers in the yard.

He woke soon after dawn. Something was resting on his foot: Jackson's head, he supposed. He sat motionless in his chair, listening to the dog's snores. The events of the previous evening slowly returned to him. It was strange no longer to be alone in the house. He winced as he remembered the donkey bite; but then, unsure if it had been real, he brought his hands up and smelt them. They were sharp with vinegar. So I didn't dream it, he thought.

The boy had done well not to cry. That vinegar will help, though only if his sister lets him keep it on. He tried to picture her, but found he was picturing Lynn instead. The boy's face, meanwhile, was clear in his mind.

He shifted in his chair. Jackson's snores ceased for a few moments before restarting. Wide awake now, he looked through the window at the quickening sky. He remembered how the dawn air had used to mix with the smell of disinfectant from the milking parlour. For a moment it seemed as real as the chair beneath him, and he felt a surge of well-being flow into every part of him. But then the reality of the empty stalls returned to him, along with the hollowness of the milk tank and the silence he would find out there. There may at last be a boy on the farm, only now there's nothing left to teach him.

5

The old man paused what he was doing which, confusingly given the heat, was splitting logs into kindling with a hatchet. Grace had watched as he knelt and tapped away with the blade, until an opening appeared and the wood divided along its length, always running with the grain. His hair, which was usually swept back, fell forward about his face as he looked down and concentrated. His glasses too were edging down his nose, and every now and then he pushed them back into place with the back of his hand, the hatchet coming to within inches of his face.

He straightened up. 'Whereabouts is it?'

'In the field beyond the grain bins,' said Grace loudly. Speaking like this when talking to him had already become second nature to her; it gave their conversations a surreal, slow motion quality. 'It's just lying there, the poor thing. Its leg looks horrible.'

She'd been out for a walk when she'd heard a noise coming from the crop. It had sounded something like breath coming and going, and moving quietly forward she'd followed it. There before her, lying a short way into the barley, had been a small fox. Its tongue hung out as it panted in the heat. Grace had stood completely still as she looked at it: unlike the drab creatures she'd sometimes seen in London, the colours on this one were as vivid as anything you might find in a child's picture book. Immediately she'd wanted to reach out and stroke it. It was then that she'd caught the strange smell, and saw the leg protruding from under its body. The paw had gone; all that remained was a chewed and bloody stump. She'd watched the animal pant for a moment longer before rushing back to the farmhouse.

The old man put down the hatchet and went inside. When he returned he had a rifle over his shoulder.

Grace stared at him.

'What are you doing?'

'The animal's in pain. The sooner we deal with it the better.'

'What do you mean, "deal with it"? It needs a vet, not a gun!'

The old man looked at her. He was still wearing his glasses, and sometimes, because of the reverse magnification of the lenses, his eyes looked smaller than they really were.

This was one of those times. It made him look so old that it was always a relief when he took them off, and she could see that his eyes weren't as sunken as they appeared.

'There's no use fetching a vet for a wild thing like that. A bullet's the best we can do for it.'

'You can't shoot it just because it's got a hurt leg! I've seen dogs with three legs before. If you can help me bring it back here then I can look after it.'

'This is a fox we're talking about. It's not some pet you can take care of. It'd sooner go mad than get better if you tried keeping it shut away.' He paused. 'Sounds like it's got itself caught up and chewed itself free. I'll bet it smells a fair bit?' Grace didn't reply. 'Well, chances are that'll go bad, and when it does that's a long way to die.' He seemed to be examining Grace's face to see if his words were having any effect. 'Now are you going to show me so we can get this done?'

She shook her head. 'No. There has to be a better way.'

The old man didn't move. Grace turned and walked away, leaving him behind her.

When she arrived back at the field, the fox was exactly as she'd left it. Again she found herself captivated by its colourings. 'You're beautiful,' she said quietly. The creature's flank moved rapidly up and down as it watched her, matching exactly each breath it took. 'You need to get out of the sun, don't you? But you can't because of your leg.' She'd always thought of foxes as being the size of a dog, but this one was more like the size of a cat. 'You're just a young one, aren't you?' she murmured as she stepped closer. She reached down, intending simply to lift the creature up and carry it to where there was some shade. Instantly the fox's ears flattened against its head; it drew back its lip and bared its teeth. Grace stood back, alarmed. A minute later she tried again but was met by the same response. 'I'm trying to help you,' she said, feeling the desperation growing. Not knowing what else to do but unwilling to admit defeat, she brought water in a dish from the farmhouse and set it down as close to the fox as she dared. She stood by, waiting for it to drink. She waited and waited, but all it did was watch her as it continued to pant.

That night neither she nor the old man mentioned the fox. In the morning she was up early, and she hurried up the farmyard. At first she thought the fox was asleep, but then she saw how still its flank was, and how the flies had settled around its eyes. The smell was stronger, and she picked up the dish from yesterday and emptied it. She stood up to go but then reached forward and stroked the orangey head.

Back at the farmhouse she found the old man splitting more wood. He stopped as she approached, but she walked past him without a word. She went upstairs; Billy's bed was empty, and she sat down on her own bed and cried. When it had passed she took her mobile phone from the drawer and returned downstairs. Stepping outside, she stood there until the old man noticed her.

'I'm sorry,' she said. 'I should have listened to you yester-day.'

The old man gave the faintest of nods. 'It dead?'

'Yes.'

'You weren't to know. These things take learning. Truth is that leg mightn't have been the whole story.'

They stood there in silence for a time.

'Your mother was the same, you know.'

Grace frowned. 'She was?'

The old man nodded. 'Never liked killing. Not for any-thing, not even when that was the kind thing to do. Times were she'd not speak to me for days afterwards.' He worked his jaw and looked away. 'It happened often enough that I don't think she much liked me in the end.'

Grace stared at him. The seconds passed as she thought about how little Lynn had mentioned him over the years.

'Will you help me bury it?' she said.

'Bury it?' The surprise in the old man's voice was clear. 'There's no use digging a hole for a fox. The flies'll soon see to it. That won't take long in this heat.'

Grace thought of the fox lying alone in the field, and felt the tears coming again. Her grip on her mobile phone tightened.

'Is it all right if I use the telephone then?' She paused. 'If it's not too much trouble.'

The old man's shoulders rose and fell as he took a breath.

'Who is it you want to talk to? One of your friends?'

She nodded.

'What about that?' he said, seeing her phone. 'That's one of those things you can use anywhere, isn't it?' Without waiting for her to answer he went on, 'I've seen people use them, but I didn't know children had them as well.'

'No reception,' said Grace, ignoring her sense of wounded pride at being called a child.

'Anywhere but here then, is it?'

'Something like that.'

The old man put down the hatchet and moved past her towards the door. Again she wondered why he was chopping wood. The winter felt far off, so far off that it might never come again. She tried to remember what a cold wind felt like on her face, but couldn't summon it up. That feeling when your nose went numb. It didn't seem possible that she would ever experience it again. Not here. Such things simply couldn't happen somewhere so dusty.

She followed the old man into the kitchen and watched him lift down the phone. It hadn't rung since they'd arrived, but she'd seen it up there on the shelf next to the stove, jet black and old, with one of those circular dials and a spiral cord. She'd been looking at it hopefully for days, but now, after what had happened with the fox, she felt the need to talk to someone more sharply than ever. She pictured Alice's mobile ringing, and how her friend would look at the strange number and then decide whether or not to answer it.

The old man bent down, his hands on his knees, so that his face was level with the phone. He blew. Fetching a tea towel from where it hung on the rail of the stove he wiped off what dust was left. Thin streaks of moisture remained from his spit. Lifting the receiver he listened for a moment before replacing it. 'Well now,' he said, 'that's a job to say.' He handed it to her.

Grace held the receiver to her ear. The dialling tone was faint, and she had to concentrate to hear it, like she was trying to detect a weak pulse. She nodded at the old man. Raising his eyebrows he stayed where he was, as if waiting for some kind of proof. It was only as Grace continued to look at him that he turned to go.

Ten minutes later Grace stood by the stove in much the same manner, as if she too was still waiting for something to happen. But there was no more to come – the conversation was over. Only it hadn't really been a conversation at all: for every ten words that were spoken, fewer than half were heard. It was as if they had been shouting at each other through a wall of some kind, a wall constructed from all those miles of distance that lay between them. Or instead, perhaps it was the silence of the farmhouse that was simply too overwhelming for little things like words to survive long enough to be heard. Yes, she thought as she stood there, feeling it creeping in through her skin, seeping through her pores and into her blood, it's the silence. She looked around the kitchen and through the window at the motionless leaves on the trees, seeing it everywhere; until, at last, the tap-tap-tap of a hatchet on wood reached her from outside.

Billy pushed the stock hard in against his shoulder and cheek. With one eye shut he looked along the barrel, lining up the sights the way the old man had shown him. He curled his finger around the trigger and tried to breathe slowly and calmly. He said the words to himself as he did it: slowly, breathe in – and calmly, breathe out. Slowly, and calmly. The old man was right: it helped.

The gun was still a bit rusty, but between them they had scraped off the worst with a wire brush. Billy had found it tucked in against one of the barns' metal uprights, half hidden by old spiders' webs. The barrel had been brown and rough to the touch, and to begin with he'd thought it was made of wood. But when he picked it up and felt the weight of it, he knew. It was a real gun.

He'd spent the rest of that morning ambushing imaginary enemies around the farm. Because his leg still hurt, he pretended he was wounded. I'm like a veteran, he told himself, though he wasn't exactly sure what that was. He was pretty sure it involved being wounded though, and being strong and brave enough to fight on, and so he exaggerated his limp to prove it. So preoccupied was he with an assault on some straw bales that he didn't see the old man until he was nearly upon him. Instantly all the fun went out of the game. It was over; he had been spotted.

'Where did you find it?' said the old man, taking the gun from him.

'In the barn,' said Billy, his voice barely audible, his head down. The old man looked questioningly at him. '*In the barn*,' he said again, overly loudly and with exaggerated mouth movements.

The old man turned the gun over in his hands. He rubbed at the rusty barrel and then the wooden stock, which was already coming up from being handled. He shook his head.

'It's a lot of years since I saw this thing.' He looked back at Billy. 'Which barn?'

Encouraged by the absence of anger in the old man's voice, Billy said, 'The one with all the buckets. And the metal things down the middle.'

'With the chalk writing on the walls?'

Billy nodded.

'That's the old calf shed.' He looked again at the gun, as though hoping to remember. 'Must've been shooting rats and left it there. They used to come in after the feed. Leave anything out and they'll find it. And if they're hungry enough there's nothing they won't eat.'

'It was pushed into a corner,' said Billy, eagerness replacing his guilt now that he didn't appear to be in trouble. 'The gun was. It was covered in cobwebs but I pulled it out.'

The old man nodded. And then, to Billy's amazement, he handed the gun back to him.

'Stay here,' he said.

With the old man gone, and with the gun still in his possession, Billy had felt like he'd never felt before. The idea of running around and making shooting noises now seemed childish and silly to him; not only was he holding a real gun, but a gun that had been used to kill rats. He looked down as he cradled it. This thing had achieved what he had long since given up trying to do with stones. It had ended one of those slithering, scuttling lives.

The old man wasn't long. Along with the wire brush, he brought with him a round tin. The word WASP was written in large print across its lid. Billy stared at it where it lay on the ground while the old man worked on the rust.

'Well now,' said the old man under his breath, 'let's see how you are inside.' He straightened up, and Billy watched as he snapped the gun in two, breaking the barrel downwards. For a moment he was torn between anger that he'd done it and admiration that he was strong enough to.

The old man ran one of his fingers over the break, and Billy saw that he hadn't broken it all. The metal was squared off, and a mechanism held the two pieces together.

'Not too bad,' murmured the old man, the words hardly leaving his mouth. He pointed at the tin on the ground. 'Open that up and give me one.'

The tin was much heavier than Billy had expected, and when he turned it over it rattled like a box of marbles. He unscrewed the lid and found it was full of little metal pellets.

They smelt like the tubs of engine oil he'd found in one of the sheds.

He watched as the old man loaded the gun and brought the barrel back up into position. Then, aiming at a piece of wood that was leaning against the same straw bales that Billy had been attacking earlier, and using a knot of darker wood as a target, he fired. A lighter spot appeared near the centre of the knot. He reloaded, showing Billy how it was done.

And now, remembering what he had learnt, Billy's finger tightened on the trigger. Tighter, then tighter still, increasing the tension by fractions as he remembered the old man's instructions. He held his breath, and the gun sprang to life.

The rat jumped, then ran a few yards. Billy's heart accelerated: he'd hit it. But then he watched as the rat continued to nose about in the dust. The only indication that he'd hit it was when every so often it looked to lose its balance, and it scurried for another few feet with a sideways gait before stopping again.

He stood the gun on the ground, stock first, and using all his weight prised the barrel down. The old man had done this in his hands, but the spring in the mechanism was too strong for Billy. So the old man had told him to do it like this, and with a great effort he could just manage it.

He felt around in his pocket and brought out a pellet. They were oddly soft: when the old man had told him to aim for the 'o' in Massey Ferguson on one of the old bits of machinery, and afterwards they had gone to look (a chip in the paint right beside the 'o' marked the spot), he had found the pellet lying on the ground. It was flat and nearly unrecognisable.

He snapped the gun shut and got back into position. The rat was crouched side-on to him, and he took aim. His heart thumped in his chest, and again he concentrated on his breathing to steady himself.

This time when he pulled the trigger the rat squealed and fell onto its side. By the time he got there it had gone quiet, and he guessed it was dead. But when it saw him it began to try to drag itself away using only its front feet. He stood over it and watched. There was a drop of blood on its back, dark and pure-looking. The pellet had done something to it that meant nothing behind its front legs would work. It continued to try to drag itself forwards, but its paws scrabbled uselessly at the dust, making a small indentation that only further impeded it. The drop of blood ran down its flank into the dirt. It was immediately replaced by another, and then another.

Standing there, Billy could hear the creature's breaths coming short and fast. It looked up at him with dark, beady eyes. He returned its look, transfixed by the life he could see in it, and by the fear in its eyes. Never before had something been so afraid of him. He wondered if it was about to die, and if he would see its eyes dim when it happened. Apart from insects he'd never seen anything die before. But for a while it just lay there, panting and bleeding, before starting to struggle again. This time it managed to pull itself along for a few inches, but before long it was out of breath. It lay still.

Billy reloaded. Standing over the rat he lowered the tip of the barrel and prodded it with it. It wasn't as interesting when it didn't move. The rat turned its head and tried to bite the metal, briefly showing its teeth. He prodded it again, wanting another look. But by now the animal was exhausted, and even when he pushed the barrel against the wound on its back it didn't respond in any more satisfying a way than with the weakest of flinches.

He moved the gun barrel up to its head. Only its whiskers were moving now, along with the occasional flick of its eyelid when the barrel got too close. He knew it was dying, but even so he pulled the trigger. A puff of dust rose. When he looked again the rat's head had crumpled, its skull knocked out of shape by the pellet at such close range. The bright little eye that had been watching him a second ago was nowhere to be seen.

He reached down and picked it up by the tail, his skin creeping at the rubbery scaliness of it. It was heavy for a dead thing; he had expected there to be less of it now that it wasn't breathing. Then, swinging it in one hand and with a feeling of satisfaction spreading through him, he walked out of the barn.

*

Grace was passing the big barn when she saw him. As well as the airgun he looked to be carrying something else. Her heart sank when she realised – from his proud walk as much as from the limpness of whatever it was – that he must have succeeded at last in killing something. Since finding the airgun he'd talked of nothing else, even to the point of no longer asking her where the television was. She was angry with the old man, not only for allowing Billy to use the gun whenever he liked but also for the encouragement. 'You can never kill enough rats,' she had overheard him saying the other evening, as he wrapped yet another vinegar-soaked cloth around Billy's leg; 'even if you could manage a thousand a day it wouldn't be enough.' And so she was left wondering why he was so intent on turning her brother into a killer, and what good he thought those stinking rags would do.

'See?' said Billy as he drew nearer. He held the rat higher for her to look. Some of its head appeared to be missing, and blood dripped from its nose or mouth.

'Why did you do it?' she said.

He looked at her and then the rat, then back at her again. 'It's a rat.'

'But why did you kill it? What did it ever do to you?'

He frowned. 'It never *did* anything to me, but they're horrible.' He remembered something the old man had said before. 'And they eat everything, so you have to kill them to stop them. And there's disease as well.' Apparently noticing her reluctance to look at it he continued, 'It only looks like

88

that because I had to shoot it twice. Actually three times, the first time didn't really—'

'Okay, enough,' she said, raising her hands. The two of them stood there in silence. 'So why are you touching it if it's got a disease?' Grace asked. 'Are you taking it somewhere?'

Billy looked at his hand, as if he might be able to see if any disease had got onto it. 'It's okay to touch them when they're dead; it's only when they're alive that you, that they …' Grace watched as he double-checked his hand. 'It's different when they're dead.'

'So where are you taking it?'

Billy thought for a moment. He hadn't really known where he was going with it; he'd just wanted to carry it around for a bit to prove his success. He shrugged. 'Don't know. Probably back to the house. I might try and get another one first though.' The idea pleased him: if he could take two back to show the old man then that would be even better. Yes, he thought, excited now, that's what I'll do. I'll try and shoot another.

Grace was shaking her head. 'Why do you want to hurt things all the time? Why can you never just leave things alone?' She searched his face for an answer, but he only looked blankly back at her. 'This is the countryside, where animals *live* – don't you see it's their home more than it is ours? I don't like rats either but it's not like they're doing you any harm, is it?' She took a breath. 'I don't know, maybe it's because you're a boy, but haven't you had enough of –' she

89

paused, knowing she shouldn't say it, '– of death and dying? Well, *haven't you?*' she shouted after him.

But Billy was already walking away from her, back towards the barn. He suddenly looked very small, and she immediately felt bad for saying it. It's true though, she thought. Even after what's happened all he wants to do is destroy everything.

She watched his retreating figure, and wondered what was going through his mind. If she regularly doubted her own reaction to what had happened on the beach – the beach that she alone was responsible for them being on – she also doubted if he even understood that Lynn and Michael were gone for ever. He'd been the same from the very beginning. During those first hours in the police station, he'd accepted Liz's presence without a murmur, even if she had spent much of the time standing a short distance from them, speaking into her mobile phone. Later on they'd gone for a walk. Outside, the air had felt fresher, and Grace had realised that it was the evening. The day was nearly over. Shopkeepers called over to one another as they locked up; at one point she heard Briscombe mentioned, and she saw the concern in their faces.

Billy was hungry again, and once they'd waited for Liz to finish her cigarette they went into a café. Grace got the sense that the woman behind the counter and Liz knew each other, but besides getting them their order and looking Grace and Billy over, the woman hardly said a word. 'Try and have something,' said Liz when Grace told her she wasn't hungry, and Grace had let her buy her a pastry. Shortly afterwards Billy needed to go to the bathroom. 'What's going to happen to us?' said Grace when he was gone. Liz had paused, and then simply said the same thing as she'd said earlier, accompanied by the same lipsticky smile. 'Don't worry, we're going to make sure you and your brother are looked after.' 'But how?' said Grace, not knowing how they could even go home now without Lynn and Michael. 'They're dead, aren't they?' 'We don't know anything for sure,' said Liz, her voice sharper, 'and I for one would rather deal with facts. Wouldn't you?' And then there was Billy back again.

Back at the police station they found another, older woman waiting for them. She'd looked nervous as they approached, and Grace found she could hardly breathe as she guessed what she was there to tell them. But she was wrong: Liz introduced Judith, explaining that she was a foster carer and that they were to stay at her house for the time being. Even this news Billy had accepted without a word; it was only later, as they got ready for bed surrounded by the floral wallpaper of Judith's spare room, that he became restless and started asking when they were going back to the cottage.

The house had been impossibly clean. Both supper that night and breakfast the next morning were plain but punctual. To Grace, none of it seemed real. The following day, in desperate need of some air and a break from Billy's questions, she'd slipped out for a walk. She'd already passed the post office before it occurred to her to go in. She didn't have to look for long: the papers were full of it. And so it was that when Liz arrived later in the day, Grace was already numb with the news.

No longer able to see Billy, and with no fixed idea of where she was going, Grace turned and carried on up the farmyard. All she wanted to do was walk. The heat shimmered over the open fields before her. She tried to concentrate on it, but when she blinked back the tears and looked again, there were only fields. They were dead because of her – of that she had no doubt. And now she and Billy were on a farm in the middle of nowhere, something that once again she alone was responsible for.

She could remember the conversation she'd had after-wards with Liz nearly word for word. With their parents gone, there was the question of where she and Billy would live. Although imagining any kind of future without Lynn and Michael had seemed impossible, the prospect of living with Judith in her spotless house had forced Grace to think quickly. So she told Liz about their grandfather, taking care to omit the fact that they'd only met him once when they were younger. Liz had nodded, as if, Grace thought, she'd been waiting for her to say this, and had an answer already prepared. She was right. 'I can understand that you want to be with your own family, and where possible it's something we do our best to facilitate,' she said. 'However, it isn't always the best solution – in fact children often find that after the inevitable period of adjustment they're actually happier in a foster home than they might have been with a relation.' Liz had paused, perhaps waiting for a response. When Grace said nothing she glanced down at her notes, shuffling through the loose sheets of paper as she searched her own handwriting. 'But tell me, is your granddad the only family you have? I thought maybe there was someone else.' Grace had shaken her head. 'No. There's only him. My father's parents died years ago.' 'Oh,' said Liz, looking up and smiling that familiar, meaningless smile. 'Sorry. I must have imagined it.'

The whole idea of fostering was repulsive to Grace. She'd noticed how careful Liz always was to call them foster carers, but it was clear what would be expected of Billy and her. After this 'period of adjustment' they'd be encouraged to think of these people as their parents. Over time, they'd be expected to love them the same as they'd loved Lynn and Michael. And what if they didn't? What if their new parents were unprepared for Billy's behaviour? Would they be passed on to the next family? Or would Liz and the people she worked for decide that Billy needed special care, leaving her in one place and sending him to another?

There was something else, something besides her fear of fostering. Her memory of her grandfather was hazy (Billy didn't remember him at all; 'Well, try to imagine you can,' Grace had whispered to him one evening at Judith's house, 'and if anyone asks, say that you like him very much') but over the years the farm he lived on had grown in her mind, until it came to represent a kind of Eden, a giant version of Greenwich Park, only with animals instead of people. Lynn's reluctance to talk about where she grew up had only added to the intrigue.

But it soon became clear which course of action Liz considered the most appropriate. At each mention of fostering, Grace had been surprised by the conviction she could hear in her own voice. 'No,' she'd said, 'we want to be with our own family.' 'He's an old man,' Liz had replied softly, 'he lives by himself miles from anywhere. Don't you think you'd be happier in London, nearer your friends? We can arrange that.' Grace had shaken her head, confused that she should know so much about a man she knew so little about herself, but sure that her cajoling was designed to trick her. 'No,' she'd said, again and again. She and her brother wanted to be with family. They wanted to go and live with their grandfather on his farm.

And now here they were: the hoped-for had become real. How wrong she had been. Besides the wide-open space, and the trees and the birds, the farm was nothing like Greenwich Park. Instead of an oasis of peace and quiet, a place where people converged to relax and rejuvenate, here there was only emptiness. Her thoughts returned to Alice. Her voice on the phone, so faint and far away. Unless the mobile in her pocket decided to work, Billy and the old man were all she had now.

She wondered what would happen when the time came to go back to school. No one had talked about school yet.

She reached the first field and stopped near its edge. She thought of the fox's body that would still be lying in the same place, not far from where she stood. She wondered if the beautiful colours would have faded by now. Before she knew it she was walking towards the place. Bracing herself for what she might find, she hunted about at the edge of the crop. But the fox was gone; instead there was an area of disturbed earth. When she looked closer, she saw large boot prints in the soil.

She stayed as she was, running her hand over the spiky tops of the barley. She pictured the old man digging in the heat. Why hadn't he told her he'd done it? Because he knew I'd come and look for it, she thought, and immediately she felt a part of herself go out to him. She wondered how he had found it. But when she looked back at the way she'd come, she saw her own footprints leading away from her.

She liked the way the barley felt alive under her palm. Looking out, she imagined how many seeds must have been sown to get that many plants – it must be millions, billions even. She considered picking a couple and taking them to Spider's chickens, but they were such ugly birds, always pecking at each other with staring eyes and stepping in their own droppings. She didn't know why, but she'd always imagined country chickens to be friendly creatures, contented by their outdoor existence. But they were just chickens.

She turned and looked back at the buildings behind her. So much about the farm was different to what she'd expected: where were the animals, where was the hard work? It felt childish even thinking it, but where were the *tractors*? She remembered how empty it had all looked from the top of the grain bin that first day. She glanced over at them, those four silver giants that seemed so modern and out of place here.

Something occurred to her as she stood there. She started walking back towards them, and when she reached the one nearest her she stopped at the bottom of the ladder. Craning her neck back she looked up. It seemed higher than before, but this she began to see as a good thing. A thought came to her, a favourite phrase of her mother's. *There's nothing to lose in trying*.

She began to climb. The day was breathless, and she was soon sweating. She could feel the tightness of the phone in the pocket of her jeans, and the sense of it there spurred her on. She imagined how the vibrate alert would feel if it found a signal up here; she even dared to picture herself sitting at the top, reading the texts as they came in.

The climb was easier than she remembered. Perhaps it was the lack of wind or the absence of Spider standing watching her from below; or maybe it was simply because she'd done it before. Soon enough the vertical section of the ladder gave way to the sloped approach, and the next minute she was there. In her jeans the phone stayed silent.

She stood awhile and caught her breath. Taking the phone from her pocket she held it out in front of her, like a favourite racing pigeon she was preparing to release. She shaded the screen with her hand against the brightness and waited.

The view of the farm made her think again of her first time up there, and she could almost taste the newness of it all that day. The same dizziness started to creep into her too, but she just breathed and looked away, letting her eyes sweep over the tanned fields. High above, a single skylark held its position, its song filtering down to her.

Suddenly the phone came alive in her hand – or at least she thought it did, for many times afterwards she would wonder if she had imagined the vibration in her palm, had wished it into being. It took her by surprise, and instinctively she reached for the handrail for support. In that moment, in that flash of altered concentration, her grip on the phone loosened. She watched as it slipped from her hand, falling the few feet to the conical roof, where it bumped noisily onto the metal. It began to slide. Its movement was so slow and deliberate that she even had time to look ahead of it, hoping for some kind of gutter or raised rim that might catch it and halt the horror that was unfolding before her. But no such thing existed. The phone slid on, scraping its way to the edge, and was gone.

PART TWO

6

Days came and went. Each morning the sun rose and passed over the farm, stripping everything of moisture until even the ground went brittle and cracked. By night Grace and Billy slept in the same room, but as soon as the sun was up they separated, each finding their own ways to pass the time. 'What do you do all day?' Grace asked her brother, both out of a sense of duty but also out of genuine curiosity. Billy would shrug, saying little in reply. It was clear that wherever he went he always took the gun with him, and Grace had images of dozens of dead rats piled into a heap somewhere, with the old man's words about never being able to kill enough of them echoing in her brother's head as he swung yet another limp body on top. But she'd found no such heap. Some days she tried following him, but sooner or later he always disappeared. He would walk into a barn, and when she followed he would be gone. At times she even lost him out in the open: it was as if the farm swallowed him up, not leaving a trace behind.

One evening she came across the blue tin of WASP airgun pellets under his bed. It was still two-thirds full; '500' it said on the lid. Immediately, she considered hiding it. Surprised at herself, at her childishness, she searched her thoughts. Why do I want to hide it? And why, now that I think about it, is the idea of hiding the gun itself even more appealing to me? Is it only that I want to stop him killing things? She continued to mull it over, and found that she wanted to annoy him too, to make him argue with her like he used to. She wanted to be reminded of how things had been before.

It was the very next morning when she realised what had changed between them. She stood at the door of the bathroom, surveying the scene before her. Pools of water lay everywhere. Grey-brown smudges lined the edge of the bath itself, evidence of the struggle she'd just lost. I'm doing my best, she thought to herself, I can't do any more. And then she saw it: she'd traded her role as sister for that of mother, and it was a role in which she was failing.

She started sleeping late. She would wake to find Billy's bed empty, and the sun hard at the window. Any colour had long since been bleached from the curtains, and the light passed through virtually unhindered. She wasn't even sure why she bothered drawing them each night. Some mornings she would lie there for hours, listening to the birds outside. It seemed strange to her that they should still be singing, to be carrying on as usual after what had happened; just as she had expected a greater change in herself, so she expected the things around her to acknowledge that life would never be the same again. But the birds don't care, she told herself. They don't even know about it. On those rare days when she could hear the turning of leaves in the trees, she thought the same thing about the wind, wondering how it could still blow the same as ever. Only the silence and the stillness of the nights felt in any way appropriate.

She spent hours thinking about her old life. They'd stopped in Greenwich for an hour on the way here: time enough to pack some things but no more. Liz had wanted it that way. 'We need to keep you and your brother looking forwards, not backwards,' she had said. She was the same at the funeral, only allowing them to stay for a short time afterwards. Remembered now, it made Grace angry, with Liz but also with herself for not resisting harder. The truth was she'd been in no state to argue. All those hugs she received from friends of the family had only made it worse; each one had felt like a goodbye of its own. Even Alice, who could normally make anything seem better than it really was, had struggled to say anything at all, preferring to hold her as they cried into each other's hair. And all the while Billy had stood beside Liz, watching from a distance.

Now Grace spent hours mentally walking through their old home. She could remember everything perfectly. Even the tiniest details remained, from spots where the carpet was a little worn to the click of a door closing, or what the rain sounded like on the roof above her bedroom. There were those things she wished they'd brought with them, such as her books and the television – for now she found it was she who wanted to sit before her favourite programmes, and give herself over to the familiarity they would offer. She wished too that she'd brought more reminders of their parents, though the two framed photographs they did have were tucked away in Billy's suitcase. It had been too upsetting to have them out. And yet when she came across Lynn and Michael on these mental walks through her old house, it had the opposite effect. The mere sight of her mother, glimpsed through the partition door that separated the sitting room from the kitchen, was nearly enough to lull Grace back to sleep. Viewed from behind as he sat working in his study, her father's image was of equal comfort to her. Imagined like this her parents were as alive as they had ever been, but to look at their photographs, with their posed smiles preserved behind glass, was to acknowledge the finality of their absence.

One thing she had brought with her was clothes, even if most days she wore the same thing: a T-shirt and some denim shorts cut as short as possible from a pair of jeans. She soon stopped bothering with underwear. Everything had to be hand-washed (this she did in the bath, every few days because of the dust, placing the wet clothes in the sun afterwards to dry) and it was too hot for wearing bras anyway. Without the envy of her friends, and with no one around but the old man and her brother, and occasionally Spider, there seemed little point in worrying about appearances.

Other mornings she would just lie there, not knowing what there was to get up for. Out in the farmyard there were only memories of her smashed phone, the loss of which she still replayed over and over in her head. Finally hunger would drive her downstairs. Eating became a kind of ritual: as she ate so she thought, and in the silence of the farmhouse the sound of her own chewing became vital to the process, as if her jaw was pedalling her brain. In turn the food she ate took on a new importance: each mouthful, it seemed to her, contained the seed of a thought or idea, and the act of swallowing started the process of germination. Even the apparent randomness of what she could find in the kitchen seemed significant. Sometimes there would be meat in the fridge, wonderful, blood-red meat, often still on the bone, which the old man would cook that evening and would then last them cold for days. (When asked what it was and where it came from, the old man told them it was venison, and that it came from 'around about'; not knowing what venison was, Grace contented herself that it tasted a lot like beef.)

Only in the evening did the three of them spend any

time together. It was also when they ate vegetables from the little patch outside next to the donkey paddock. The old man had shown Billy how to dig them – always Billy, Grace noticed, never her, even though she was the one who not only knew about vegetables but also enjoyed eating them. When he was first entrusted with digging them by himself, she had readied herself for disaster. (Once, Lynn having left the room briefly while making a tomato sauce, he had managed not only to cut his finger with the knife on the chopping board, but also to then stir a quantity of his own blood into the sauce itself, making it taste oddly metallic; the fact that he waited until they were eating it before telling them only further exasperated their parents.) But on this occasion, and to her unending surprise, he'd returned with a handful of leeks, already trimmed and peeled, the unwanted bits left in the paddock for Easter and Jenny. Other than the soil on his hands and under his fingernails, he was unmarked.

Some days she would wake to the smell of freshly baked bread, and come down to find a pair of loaves cooling across their tins on the stove. Dense and heavily seeded, it was unlike any bread she'd eaten before. Buttered while still hot, a slice beneath one of Spider's eggs, which she boiled, made the best breakfast imaginable. Those were the good days. At other times the bread bin would be empty, the egg tray too, and she would have to make do with whatever old crusts Billy hadn't found earlier that morning. These fluctuations

106

were mirrored nearly to perfection by her mood, and so conscious did she become of this that she soon began to believe utterly that she was indeed what she ate.

Afterwards, wearing the flip-flops bought for her the very day it happened (this a daily reminder that both pained and reassured her) she would step outside. Feeling the heat first on her bare skin – her face, her arms, her legs – soon it encased her completely. All she would hear were the birds in the trees and crickets calling from the uncut lawn. Before long her feet would be coated in dust, blending with the deeper tan of her legs. Day after day she had the same thought: surely this relentless heat was proof of global warming. She wished it would rain, if only so that something would change. And then, standing there by herself she would wonder where everyone was. The old man was probably asleep somewhere, and Billy – well, Billy could be anywhere. She would contemplate trying to find him, but already her energy would be dissipating, evaporating under the sun. And anyway, she would reason to herself, as the prospect of stretching out on a blanket in the grass for a couple of hours hung before her, I'll only run into Spider. I always do.

From the pit the old man released the gate. On one side above him the cattle filed out into the darkness. Walking to the other end he let the next batch in, calling out over the noise of the machines when the lead animal baulked and blocked the others. He counted them in, pulling down the bar to stop them coming, and because he had to do it quickly he caught the last animal on its haunch, making it push forward onto its neighbour and causing a commotion that spread along all eight of them. Their hooves clattered on the concrete as they jostled, slipping and skidding in the wet mix of mud and shit before they settled. Feed shot down into the troughs as they found their places. Working around their hind legs, his own head not much higher than their hocks, the old man got busy. Beyond the bar, standing flank to flank, the rest of the animals watched, waiting their turn.

It'll freeze again tonight, he thought, though surrounded by this lot you'd never know it. Even the metal's warmer to the touch in here. If only I could harness their heat instead of letting it escape up through the roof. He smiled to himself as he thought it: milk, meat, leather – and now heat. He listed the other uses while he worked. There was tallow for making soaps, and candles too in the old days. Gelatin. Then there was glycerine. They made gunpowder out of glycerine.

The dream moved on. He was outside the milking parlour, his breath showing against the dark sky. The mud was already hardening underfoot, and beneath the lights of the barn the cattle tossed steaming silage over their shoulders as they ate. Some were already in the barn itself, lying on a fresh bed of straw. The pleasure he took from seeing them there, warm and dry on a cold night such as this, was as strong as ever.

But then he caught the scent of it on the night air. Looking closer he saw that some of what he'd thought was steam was smoke; one or two of the animals were smouldering. The smell of burnt hair reached him again through the frost. Then came the flames. They were small at first, little orange creatures that danced around their hooves, but as he watched they seemed to breed, to divide and divide again, spreading from cow to cow. The animals were becoming restless, and the old man hurried across the yard, desperate to shut them out of the barn, away from the straw. He was nearly at the gate when one of them, with the flames twisting hungrily up its legs, broke into a run, bucking and kicking as it tried to throw off the pain. His hand was on the gate when it passed him, and he heard the flurry of flames as it went.

The fire spread quickly after that. The straw took to the flames instantly, as if it had harboured a desire for heat ever since the warm days of harvest. Soon the barn was alight, the concrete and metal sections standing by as everything else was consumed. He tried to let the cows out into the yard, but they too were alight, and he stood back afraid. He watched one animal run around in circles, bellowing in pain before him, its eyes wide and rolling as the fire ate at it. Finally it disappeared around the corner of the barn, leaving a trail of smoke hanging in the air behind it.

He retreated, driven back across the yard by the heat. He was breathing hard, but his breath no longer showed against the sky. And although his was the only face looking up at the blaze, and although there was a smell of burning flesh in the air, before he woke it was as if the grandest Guy Fawkes bonfire in the east had been lit in his farm-yard.

Grace came downstairs to find the old man unpacking bags of food in the pantry. The farmhouse door was open, and there outside was the blue Ford she'd seen parked in one of the barns. She watched the old man continue to unload the bags with annoyance.

'I said I wanted to come with you,' she said.

'If there's anything you want you can tell me and I'll soon get it,' said the old man without looking up.

'You don't understand. There are things only I can get.'

'What things?'

Grace took a breath.

'Women's things.'

The old man looked at her, and she wondered if he had any idea what she was talking about.

'Oh,' he said. Again he was silent for a time. 'How soon do you need them?'

'Soon.'

The old man nodded.

'It's been a long while since there was any call for things

like that in this house. That's town you'll need, not the village. I'll drive you in this afternoon.'

It took much longer to get there than Grace expected. The old man drove so steadily that she was hardly aware of when he was accelerating or braking. She and Billy sat in the back seat. She thought of the last time they were in a car together like this, and she reached over and put her hand on his. After only a short time he moved his away.

The first houses started to appear, and very soon afterwards the old man turned into a market square. A row of shops stood at each end, and what looked like an old wooden bandstand served as a kind of centrepiece. Grace caught her breath when she saw the same bank and shop names she was used to seeing in London.

The old man reversed into a parking space and switched off the engine. He sat there, staring through the windscreen. Grace too stayed as she was, giving herself a moment to calm.

'We used to come here,' said the old man. 'For a lot of years we did. On market day. All this,' he nodded at the wide, empty space before him, 'you couldn't move for animals.'

Grace waited. Beside her Billy looked out of the window, and then she realised something.

'I don't have any money.'

The old man continued staring straight ahead. 'From here clear across to the other side,' he said. 'The noise – you can't imagine the noise.' He took a long, slow breath. 'I can hear it now.'

'I said I don't have any money,' said Grace, louder this time. She glanced across at Billy, but his attention too seemed held by what was outside the car.

'On you go, then.'

Looking up, Grace saw the old man watching her in the rear-view mirror. He held a hand aloft, and in it was a crumpled note. She paused, stilled by the sensation of watching herself from afar, the same as she'd experienced that day on the beach.

'Isn't it enough?'

'Yes, yes thank you, it's more than enough,' she said, and reaching forward she took it from him.

The chemist was on the opposite side of the square. As Grace hurried over the cobbled ground she tried to picture it filled with animals. But she couldn't, mostly because she didn't know what kinds of animals she should be imagining. Passing the wooden bandstand she heard voices; above her, leaning and sitting on the railings, were half a dozen boys and girls her own age. A couple of them held bags of chips, and she caught the smell of vinegar that came from them.

'All right?' said one of the boys when he saw her. The others all stopped what they were doing and looked down at her. Their attention was so sudden that she passed quickly on.

Inside, the chemist was nearly identical to the one back in Greenwich. She soon found what she was after, and she was on her way out when she stopped before the doors and tried imagining she was back in London. It didn't take much. She looked again at the doors: to get home, all I need do is go out, turn right and then follow the road round towards the university. She stood awhile, letting the sense of peace the idea brought wash over her. But then she thought of the old man and Billy waiting in the car.

Back out in the square, she walked once more towards the wooden bandstand. The same children were there, and as she drew nearer she saw that one of the girls was busy keying a message in on her mobile phone. When she reached the group she stopped. She was aware that the others had fallen silent and were looking at her, but it was only when the girl glanced up from her phone that anyone said anything.

'What?'

Grace smiled at her. 'I just wanted to say hi,' she said. 'I had a phone like that but it broke.'

The girl frowned. 'So why are you telling me?'

'Where are you from?' asked one of the boys. 'You sound posh.'

'London.'

'London? What are you doing here then?'

Grace paused. 'I – I don't know.'

'What d'you mean you don't know?' said the girl.

Grace looked at her. 'I suppose I'm on holiday.'

'On holiday?' said one of the other boys. 'Here? That's fucked.'

The other two boys laughed, and when, out of relief, Grace laughed too, she sensed their eyes on her.

'What's so funny?' said the girl. 'You think you're better than us because you live in London?'

'No, of course not, I—'

'I went to London once and it's a shithole.' The girl spat out the word as if it tasted bad. 'Yeah? What d'you think of that?'

Grace tried to think of something to say as the girl stared at her. Beside them the boys fidgeted and looked around.

'What's in the bag?' said the girl.

Grace glanced down at where it swung from her hand. 'Oh, nothing. Just some things for my granddad.'

The girl was still looking at the bag. When she raised her head, something in her face had changed.

'Yeah?'

Grace nodded.

'He gets a lot of periods, does he?'

There was a moment's silence as the rest of the group focused on the plastic bag, and then the laughter started. Grace backed away, and then quickly started walking towards where the blue Ford was parked. Getting in, she pushed the bag under the seat in front of her.

'Get everything you need?' said the old man.

'Yes.' Through the windscreen she could still see the group laughing and looking their way.

'That's good. I was now telling your brother about market day, and how we used to come here. This whole square—'

'Can we go now?' said Grace.

The old man was quiet. The faint jingle of keys reached the back seat, and then the Ford shook to life.

7

Slipping inside and resting against the wall, Billy waited for his eyes to adjust to the shade. He moved slowly, something he had learnt to do over the last few weeks. You saw a lot more that way. Rats, he had discovered, really couldn't see that well.

He had slowed down in other ways too. Now when he was asked something, he considered his answer thoroughly before speaking, turning the question over in his head the way the old man did. When he did answer, he chose his words carefully, wanting to be as accurate with them as he'd become with the airgun. Some days he didn't speak at all until the evening, when he returned to the farmhouse; it seemed to him a waste to say just anything, to scatter words about like he'd seen the strange man Spider throw grain for his chickens. As those long, silent days drew to a close and he was required to say something, his voice would croak, his vocal chords dry from disuse. It made him sound older, which he liked. He felt older.

Another difference in him was when he was faced by a problem. Instead of acting on the first idea that presented itself, now he waited for a time to see if another might appear. Perhaps the biggest change of all was that he'd stopped running. He'd given it up. The same thought occurred to him time and again, reinforced by his new sense of control: I wasn't built for running. I don't know exactly why (although, because of a pain he got if he crouched for too long, he suspected his knees were to blame), but that's the reason I was never any good at football. It wasn't that they were any better than me, those other boys; it was more that their legs were better made for running. So now he walked, he crept, he stalked, and by rolling his feet from heel to toe he found he could move almost without a sound.

He looked up, seeing the flashes of white in the rafters. Once his eyes had fully adjusted he saw the way their heads moved about, turning from side to side to get a better look at him. They were right to be nervous: he'd already killed nearly thirty, and five of those had come today, with only seven shots. He wondered why they were so reluctant to move. Occasionally one or two dropped from the rafters and flew outside, but mostly they just stayed and watched as he

117

shot at them. Perhaps it's all that sky, he thought, perhaps there's too much of it. All that sky and all that sun.

It was the old man who had told him to look up. Billy had tilted his head back and looked until his neck hurt. There were dozens of them, each returning his gaze. It nagged at him that they'd been there all the time, watching him from the rafters as he came and went, watching him chase and kill rats, and run and trip and fall. All the time he had thought he was alone they had been there, watching.

'We were given them years ago, back when your grandmother was still alive,' said the old man when he asked about them. 'They were all white back then, mind. She used to like to see them. So long as they stayed, the farm and all those who lived and worked on it would be blessed. That's what she said.' He'd looked up at the nests and the heads that bobbed about as they watched them. 'But that was before the racers started coming. At first we didn't mind them; we thought they was resting on their way to somewhere else. Apart from not being white, you knew they were racers because you could see the rings on their legs. Sometimes they had two or three, metal and plastic. I didn't like it when they stayed more than a few hours, or a day at most. I mean, I knew what was likely to happen. That's just the way of things. But your grandmother said it was the same as if a stranger stopped at our door, and needed somewhere to rest up for the night. "You wouldn't turn them away, would you?" she'd say to me. "You'd feed them and water them like they were your own, and let them stay until they were good and ready." That was the way of that woman, she always knew how to argue things into the light.

'But then a day turned to two, and a week later they'd still be here. I'd say to her, "That racer's still here, I think it's getting comfortable." She'd shake her head and tell me to be patient, that it'd be on its way any day now. Soon it became so that I couldn't say anything. Every time I saw the flock there it was, feeding alongside the others like it was the same as they were. Even from a distance you could see it, its dark feathers standing out among the other birds like a bit of dirt does in the snow. I knew what had to happen – even your grandmother must've known, though she never said as much – but even so, when I saw the first hybrid my heart sank. I – what's that?' Billy had said that funny word again, raising his voice. 'Hyb*rid*, not hyb*rod*,' said the old man. He'd brought out his handkerchief and wiped his nose before continuing. 'That's when two different kinds of animals breed, and produce a third kind that's neither one nor the other. Like then with that racing pigeon. It bred with a dove, and the chick they had was this mixed thing, all black and grey feathers mixed in among the white. I knew that was only the beginning, so I shot it right quick. It was then I decided to shoot the racer too. You see I couldn't have it, I couldn't have him covering more of them and colouring up the flock like that.' Though he didn't know what covering meant, Billy had nodded. 'Anyhow, later that same day your grandmother says to me, "I see that racer's gone on its way. I told you it wouldn't stop for ever." I never said a word. But she wouldn't let it alone. "I'll miss him," she said, "I was beginning to get quite fond of him." All I could do was think about the racer and his chick lying in the filth of the muck hole, and wonder how many more chicks there was up in the rafters, or eggs waiting to hatch.

'That happened quickly then. More coloureds appeared, some darker than others, and more racers came and stayed. I shot as many as I could, but there was no use to it. She – your grandmother – she still thought they were just stopping up awhile before moving on. I never could bring myself to tell her, but she must've seen the white in some of them. I think she pretended not to notice, especially when their droppings got in the cow feed, and over the straw bales. That wasn't long before she stopped taking an interest in them altogether.'

He'd shown Billy the splashes down the barn walls, and the piles of droppings on the floor. Nothing was immune: the car that they'd travelled into town in that day – even this bore white streaks across its bonnet. 'Nothing but rats with wings,' he'd said, 'that's all they are now.' The creatures in question had watched from above throughout, as though listening with interest to the explanation of their history, to how they had turned from prized livestock to vermin that ranked alongside rats. And perhaps it was this newfound understanding that made them sit tight now, committed to their fate as Billy raised the airgun to his shoulder and shot one after another. Even when he missed or a pellet passed straight through a bird's neck and flattened noisily against the metal rafter behind it, the majority of them stayed as they were. Those he killed outright nosedived to the ground, landing with a thump, their wings shuddering before lying still; those he didn't fluttered earthwards, flapping awkwardly in a cloud of dust and feathers. Still the others stayed put. If they really had been listening to the old man, and had understood him fully, then some of them were right not to worry: of all the birds Billy killed, not one was pure white. Those that were (and despite the old man's fears, there were several of them) may as well have not been there at all. The airgun sights passed harmlessly, almost blindly, over them, and onto the next. But if he caught a glimpse of black or brown, or blue or grey, even if it was a single spot on a head or the tip of a tail feather, Billy's grip on the gun tightened and his breathing slowed. As he worked (for he thought of it as a kind of work, a duty he had taken upon himself) he thought about the grandmother he had never known. From the old man's story he felt he had a sense of her, and as he took shot after shot he felt he was restoring her, building the memory that he didn't have from scratch. The more coloureds he shot the clearer she became in his mind. He kept a careful count: it was nine now today, including the one that hadn't fallen but had slumped where it was, dying in its nest.

A dove landed at his feet. It was still alive, more alive

than it should have been. He'd come to understand that for a bird to fall from the rafters it had to be hurt a certain amount. So as this one got to its feet and started to walk off, he wondered why it had fallen in the first place. But then he saw how one of its wings hung down lower than it should, the tip trailing in the dust. He trapped it under his foot. Bending down he picked it up, holding it with his fingers and thumb in what he thought of as the bird's armpits. Recently he'd discovered that if he held them there, tightly, in those little hollows, they couldn't breathe. It saved on pellets. The dove struggled, and he dug his thumb and fingers in harder. Its head went back again and again, striving for air. He waited, watching the creature's head jerk frantically back and forth before it drooped and hung down. He threw it with the others.

He stood the airgun up inside one of the metal uprights, hiding it just as the old man must have done all those years ago in the calf shed. Holding each by a wing, he collected up the dead birds and carried them out of the barn, his eyes narrowing in the brightness. A wing slid out from between the others as he walked, and one of them fell into the dust. Bending down, he regathered it. He set off again, his hands soon aching from having to hold them so tightly.

He arrived at the muck hole. Dropping the doves onto the concrete he flexed his fingers, stretching the stiffness from them. Movement from the margins of the pit caught his eye, but when he looked all he saw were the tails of rats as they disappeared into their holes amid the undergrowth. They knew by now that this boy was dangerous, but without the airgun in his hands Billy's interest was minimal. Instead he set to work throwing the doves into the putrid water, two at a time, until the pit was littered with floating bodies.

He wasn't sure why, but looking at them made him think of Grace. The other night he'd woken to find the light on; when he turned over he'd seen her lying there with one of the pictures of Lynn and Michael clasped to her chest. Her eyes were closed, but that didn't stop the tears finding their way out at the corners. She'd broken their deal: she was crying. Occasionally her whole body seemed to shake. It had seemed odd to him that the photograph had upset her: she was the one who had brought them and stood them up on the windowsill. He could remember what she'd said as she dusted the ledge with a pillowcase. 'It'll be nice to see them every day, especially before we go to sleep and when we wake up. That way we can still talk to them and include them in what we're doing. Do you understand? It'll be like they're still here, keeping an eye on us. Especially Lynn – she'd be so worried about you being on a farm, spending all day by yourself. Actually, I'm not sure she'd like it.' He'd looked at her and felt himself frowning. 'But they're not here,' he'd said. 'So even pretending doesn't make sense.' She'd looked back at him long and hard before answering. 'It's not pretending,' she'd said quietly, 'it's remembering. There's a difference.'

He rubbed at his eyes, feeling bits of sleep still encrusted in the corners. When he looked again he had to blink a few times before the sharpness returned. He felt tired in the heat, and bored now he'd dealt with the doves. He missed the sense of purpose the airgun gave him.

He was trudging back the way he'd come when he heard an engine. His first reaction was to glance upwards for a plane. He searched the sky, but soon had to look away. The noise grew louder, but by the time he'd got as far as the big barn it had stopped. He walked to the far end of the building, stopping where a line in the dust marked the end of the shade.

There, parked outside the farmhouse, was a car. He wondered if it might be Lynn and Michael, come to take them home again. Was that possible? He didn't think so. Nevertheless, the idea of leaving the farm prompted a reluctance in him, and he might have decided to hide in the barn had Grace not appeared and started hurrying towards him.

'Thank God,' she said when she reached him. She looked him over and started brushing him down. Billy pushed her hands away. Grace stopped and held him by his shoulders.

'Listen to me! You remember that woman Liz we talked to, the one with the red hair and all the necklaces? Well she's here, and if she sees you like this she'll think you're not being looked after. And you know what'll happen if she thinks that?' Billy neither nodded nor shook his head. 'It'd mean we'd have to go and live somewhere else, with people we don't know.'

'But I want to stay here. I don't—'

'Right then, so let me get these feathers off you.'

She began to brush him down again, pausing only to pick off those feathers that resisted her efforts. Billy stayed as he was. So it's not Lynn and Michael, he thought to himself, a touch disappointed.

'Your granddad said I'd find you out here.'

Grace spun around. There she was, wearing an oversized cardigan despite the heat. The familiar necklaces hung about her neck; she had on the same shade of lipstick too. Grace smiled her best smile, and tried not to think about the dried blood she'd seen on Billy's hands.

Liz returned her smile. 'I thought I'd drop in to see how you two were getting on.' She made no attempt at subtlety as she ran her eyes over them. 'I must say you look ...' Grace's heart sank as she paused. 'Well, you certainly look as if you're living the outdoor life, I'll say that.' Again she smiled, only this time Grace sensed the effort behind it. 'So. Shall we go inside and have a little chat?'

8

Grace opened her eyes and breathed. The pulses slowed and finally faded, her pelvis settling back against the ground as her muscles relaxed. She closed her eyes again, feeling the last of the pleasure ebb from her. If only there was a way to feel like this for longer, she thought as she lay there, not for hours or anything, but just for a few minutes. I don't think I could manage more than a few minutes.

She propped herself up on her elbows, quickly buttoning up her shorts. She looked at each of the upstairs farmhouse windows in turn, but saw nothing except the framed gloom of the rooms within. She knew it was unlikely anyone would be up there to see her. Billy was never in the house at this time of day, and although the old man's bedroom was next to theirs, he didn't appear to use it. The only reason he came upstairs was to shave. If she was awake in the early hours she'd hear the creak of the stairs under his weight, the effort required by this daily ritual clear in his movement. When she heard him going back down again a short time later, she imagined she could sense his relief that it was done. It was a relief she shared in, knowing that for the rest of the day the upstairs floor was hers alone. Safe in this certainty, more than once she had dared to let herself into the old man's bedroom and look around. A layer of dust covered the wooden chest that stood against the far wall. The pillows on the bed lay undisturbed. Dead flies lay scattered over the windowsill. The windows themselves were fastened shut, and because of this the room was airless.

It was in there that she'd found the only books in the farmhouse. Old hardback copies with titles like *Deciduous Trees of Great Britain & Ireland* and *Carpentry: A Beginner's Guide* stood neatly beside one another on a single shelf. There too was a stack of newspapers, a two-foot pile of something called the *Eastern Daily Press*. She wondered why he'd kept them.

In one corner there was a closet recessed into the wall, and inside she found a row of dresses. There was something hopeful about the way they hung there, as if they were waiting for their shoulders to be filled by something other than coat hangers. Tentatively she'd reached out and touched them. Their cotton was thin, their patterns faded, and she was reminded of the charity shops she'd always loved visiting in London, and of the old people who worked in them. She thought about her mother's mother, and imagined her standing before these dresses just as she was now, deciding which one to wear today. The reek of mothballs was overpowering; to Grace it was the smell of the past, and she'd shut the closet door, feeling a touch of regret that she'd intruded on something she wasn't a part of.

She'd picked out this patch of the lawn with care (Lawn? she wondered. Can it really be called that?). Jackson had his favourite places out here too, so she'd been sure to avoid them. Her spot was as hidden in the long grass as it could have been. She'd chosen it in the first week, and set about flattening down an area a little larger than herself. The blanket she'd taken off the old man's bed fitted it perfectly. Lying down she felt completely enclosed, with only the sun overhead for company, which poured its heat down into the little space and all over her. She lay there with her T-shirt rolled up and the waist of her shorts turned down, alternating between her front and her back. As the hours passed the angle changed, until her stomach and legs were laced with shadows from the surrounding grass. It was then, just as the day was beginning to cool, that a renewed sensitivity crept over her, a fresh receptiveness that was centred (which made sense to her, physically accurate as it was) at the top of her thighs. Starting off as a warm pulse, it strengthened if she encouraged it with her fingers until, at times quicker than others, she tensed up, the pulse turning to a pure heat that spread through all of her. In those few moments she felt more alive than ever, but also not quite there at all; afterwards, as it faded, it was like coming back down to the blanket and the grass, back to where gravity governed and all those other thoughts and things she knew and recognised were there waiting for her. And this was why she wished it could last for longer.

She got to her feet and looked about, feeling a little light-headed. She bent down and gathered up the blanket; on these clear days the dew came early, when it was still light. More than once she'd been caught out, the wool of the blanket taking up the moisture like blotting paper.

Back inside she had to squint to see what she was doing. The sound of the old man's snoring reached her. Certain now that she hadn't been seen, she put away the blanket. She wondered to herself what she would say if anyone did catch her doing that. Other girls at St Siskins did it sometimes, but they rarely talked about it. It was private, the most private thing imaginable. But still the question remained: if someone saw her doing it, what would she say? She flinched at the thought of it. It was too unambiguous to be mistaken for anything else; there could be no other explanation. Silently she promised herself that she'd be more careful.

She stepped back outside, closing the door gently behind her. It wouldn't be long before Billy returned from wherever he was and the old man woke, and that would be an end to her peaceful reign. The memory of Liz's visit returned to her.

Their luck was hard to believe. She considered it nearly a miracle that Billy hadn't been carrying either a dead animal or the airgun when she found them. The airgun, she'd discovered afterwards, had been tucked away just feet from them in the barn. Then there was the bite on Billy's leg. Had Liz come a week sooner he would still have been limping. As it was she didn't appear to notice what was left of the bruising, and Grace had been only too relieved when they sat down at the kitchen table, leaving his legs out of sight. His hands too, with their smears of dried blood, he'd managed to keep in his lap. For once it had seemed that she and Billy were on the same side, that he understood what was at stake. Even Liz's questions he'd answered without any reference to what he'd been killing recently.

For her part, Liz had seemed surprised more than anything. But shortly before she left, Grace thought she detected something like disappointment in her manner. That evening, and for several days afterwards, the thought had worried her. Had she and Billy been less convincing than she'd imagined? Might Liz return at any moment to take them away? But the days passed and no one came. Why else, then? Surely she couldn't have been disappointed that they seemed happy?

Her legs were stiff after so many hours inactivity, and the denim of her shorts rubbed pleasurably against the tenderness between them as she walked. A short distance up the farmyard she turned left by a wall made from red brick; she passed through an open gate, and then another, until she

130

came to the open area of concrete she'd seen from the grain bin. The sound of her flip-flops echoed against the surrounding buildings. Weeds grew up from between cracks in the cement, their leaves surprisingly green. She could feel the reflected warmth on her ankles and calves, and as she walked she imagined the soil below, the richness of it, all dark and moist thanks to its protection from the sun. She pictured the weeds' roots twisting down into the coolness while the heat raged above. Looking about she saw into low, open-sided barns. Inside there was nothing but old straw, and here and there a bucket or a length of string.

Across from her, through a gap between one of these barns and another brick wall, she could see open fields. More weeds – taller ones, some as tall as her – grew around the edges, and as she came closer she saw that another gate was hidden among them. She passed through, stepping onto a rough track. The ground was strange and uneven. Some time ago (How long? she wondered. Months? Years?) when the ground had been softer, several animals had come through here, their hooves churning up the earth. Under the sun the soil had dried, preserving the memory of them. She carried on, finding it difficult to walk on – twice she nearly went over on an ankle – until she stopped to look again. The hoof marks were large, a good deal larger than the donkeys'. Cows, she thought, knowing she was right; it must have been a herd of cows. She looked back at the concrete area, at all the open gates. Where were they now? She let her eyes run ahead of her down the track, following the rough ground. It was as if one day they had walked out and never come back. Was that it? Could that kind of thing happen on a farm? She remembered what the old man had said that day in town about the square being filled with animals. But then something else started emerging from the memory, the embarrassment she'd suffered at the hands of that girl, and she pushed it from her mind.

She walked on, her head down as she concentrated on each footstep. She'd only gone another few yards when she heard a sound that made her stop and look up. It was a sound that frightened her, and she looked quickly about. A lone hazel bush grew out of the long grass to her right, and there in its shade was a wooden box, suspended from the ground on a wire frame. Bees came and went from a hole near its base, their wings beating a steady drone on the afternoon air. She tried to remember what she knew about bees, especially what made them attack, but she couldn't think of a single thing. Moving slowly, she crept on past; she even found she was holding her breath, as if the hive was a sleeping dog that if woken might leap and bite her.

Further along the track she came to some wooden fencing, and she saw where she was. There was the donkey paddock, and after another few yards the farmhouse came into view. The donkeys themselves were nearby. They were pushing against each other, their spindly-looking legs kicking up dust as they tried to gain extra leverage. The slighter, younger one had hold of his mother by the back of her neck, and he reared up on his back legs and mounted her, his front legs spread over her back, his hooves turned inwards. Then, as Grace watched, she saw his penis, could hardly miss it all of a sudden, as it hovered between the two animals like a third creature. Half of it abruptly disappeared from view, and the younger donkey began to thrust. Grace, who had never seen anything like it before, could only stand and watch, her eyes wide in the early evening light.

Billy was on his way back towards the farmhouse. It had been a long day, and he could feel the backs of his legs had burnt. At least he'd brought some shorts with him, and hadn't had to cut up his jeans the way Grace had.

He wondered what she did all day. He knew that sometimes – especially since that funny-looking woman with the bright lips and all the necklaces and questions had come to see them – she tried following him. But she was easy to lose. Partly, he thought, as he practised rolling his feet in the dust, it was because she didn't know how to move quietly. But it was also because she never seemed to try that hard. He knew this because he would hide and wait for her to go past, and then watch as she looked about for him. But she never looked for very long. Soon enough she would drift back towards the farmhouse, swinging her arms as she went, her tanned legs moving almost as aimlessly. He wasn't sure why, but he liked deceiving her like this. Sometimes it was all he could do not to follow her, just to see how close he could get without her realising. Other times he pretended not to notice she was behind him, leading her around in circles until (he guessed) she must have thought he was mad. Once he took her on a circuit around the farm and then back to the farmhouse, where he promptly lost her, leaving her looking about with a frown on her face while he crawled away unseen through the long grass.

His favourite thing to do, however, was to lead her towards Spider. Most days he could be found near the top of the farm with his chickens, busy refilling their water or checking the wire fence. The majority of each morning was taken up as he slowly worked his way along the perimeter, his back arched over as he hooked his fingers in the wire and pulled and tested every inch. The chickens were clearly used to this and paid him little attention, although the second he stepped inside the run they would rush towards him, gathering around his boots, one or other of them squawking or raising a wing when it got caught underfoot. He scattered grain for them, which they ate greedily. When it was all gone they scratched in the dust looking for more, turning over the parched earth again and again. Now and then Spider would reach down and snatch one up (his speed hadn't gone unnoticed by Billy either); holding it under one arm, he'd open one of their wings and cut back the feathers with some scissors. Although this was a regular occurrence, each time the chicken would shriek and yell – not from any pain, it seemed to Billy, but more in outrage at being denied the right to fly. And all the while Spider's mouth twitched from the concentration.

Feeling his sister's eyes on his back, Billy would wend his way through the farm buildings as casually as possible. Concerned that she shouldn't realise what he was up to, he'd choose a new route each time, finding a fresh way to end up close to Spider and his chickens. There was no need to lead her right to him: the little man's eyes were as quick as the rest of him, and Billy knew that so long as she passed within sight he would drop what he was doing (even, on some occasions, the chicken he was holding, its wing half finished) and make his way towards her. First, though, he would see Billy, his head jerking up as the passing boy caught his eye. But beyond a brief look of recognition nothing would pass between them. It was precisely this disinterest that made the whole operation worthwhile, enabling Billy to continue on his way while Grace was waylaid. After it had happened a few times, however, when he saw him Spider would automatically look around for Grace; and soon the initial glance that passed between him and the girl's brother took on something approaching understanding. Barely the slightest nod or flinch of an eyebrow, but nevertheless a connection had been made.

On Billy would walk, until he reached a suitable place where he could hide up and watch. By this time Spider would already be out of the chicken run, and then it was only a matter of time before he was beside Grace, shifting from foot to foot. This was Billy's favourite bit: the trap was sprung, and his hands moved with excitement by his sides as he watched. That it was a trap he could reset again and again made it all the more satisfying. He'd fooled her once more, and now he could go on his way alone, safe in the knowledge that he wasn't being observed. For although he wasn't doing anything wrong (how could he when here on the farm there were no rules?), he'd come to think of solitude as his ally, as a silent partner with whom he did everything, and who accepted the changes in him unquestioningly. Before long his own loneliness came to represent the person he wanted to be, so that when he shot at something and missed, and whispered under his breath 'too high' or 'right a bit', he was whispering not only to himself but to solitude as well, his other silent self that was there with him.

Sometimes, though, he stayed and watched – at least for a time. Spider's interest in his sister never occurred to him as strange, even if it was an interest that didn't extend as far as Billy himself. For a reason he'd never given much thought to, boys had always liked her, had always wanted to be near her; Spider, although obviously older in years, was a boy too. This Billy knew from the look they shared as he walked past. It was a look between equals. And as had so often been the case – so much so that Billy barely noticed it any more – there was an immediate and instinctive indifference there that bordered on hostility.

Grace's discomfort in Spider's company was pleasingly obvious. Sometimes he could even detect the very moment when, realising that Spider had spotted her, she considered ducking back around the corner of the building she'd come from. Before they'd come here, during the summer when Grace was in the park, Billy had spent hours in the little sunroom at the back of their house, trapping flies in a glass and then wandering around with them until he found a spider's web. He would wait and watch until the spider darted from its hole and subdued them, and then turned them in silk. And so now he liked to think, *she's in Spider's web*, as it dawned on his sister that she'd been seen; for even on the rare occasion that she did turn back, Spider would only follow and catch her up. As he talked and hopped alongside her, she'd raise a hand to her face, shielding her eyes from the sun. Occasionally she glanced about, looking, Billy guessed, for him. Usually the two of them ended up over by the chickens. Spider would catch one and show it to her. Or he'd disappear into the rickety wooden shed on wheels that occupied one end of the enclosure (and which looked like a very small and very old train carriage, with miniature ramps leading up to hatches at either end), returning with an egg that he placed carefully into her hand. Billy could tell from the way he handled them how precious eggs were to him, and having eaten them himself he could see why. There were blue ones and brown ones, but they all looked the same under their shells. Their yolks were large, with only a thin layer of white. They were delicious. And so here was another reason to lead his sister to Spider: the eggs he gave her supplemented those he already gave the old man, and it was with particular relish that Billy ate these extra food rations, especially those he hard-boiled and brought with him in his pocket, feeling that he had in some way earned them.

Recently, however, something else had started happening. It was something that in turn both annoyed and confused him. Along with the showing of chickens and giving of eggs, a new activity had entered the routine. Against the wire fence, half hidden in the long, wispy grass and stray stalks of barley, leant Spider's bicycle. Billy had seen him arrive and leave on it, but it hadn't occurred to him that anyone else could use it. So when one day Grace pointed to it and said something that persuaded Spider to wheel it out, he'd watched with a burst of envy when the next minute she was astride it, the loose mudguards clanking as she rode it up and down past its beaming owner. His jealousy was such that he decided he didn't want to play this game any more: there was no pleasure to be had from watching her ride Spider's bike, her hair flowing back from her face in the otherwise still air, while he sat and sweated in his hiding place. Even the extra eggs weren't worth this. But the first day it happened something else that so confused him he decided he had to see it again.

Billy knew that when you hid and watched, most of what

138

you saw people do didn't matter. But occasionally, if you were lucky, and patient, and all those other things he'd learnt since coming to the farm, you saw something that you knew you weren't supposed to. There was the way the person looked about beforehand, or the way they hurried off afterwards. Sometimes they slowed down as they did the actual doing, like Grace when she lay down in the grass.

So the bike rides continued. At first Grace stayed close by, circling the chicken run under Spider's gaze, but gradually her orbit grew until it included the whole farmyard, and then beyond. When she disappeared from view Billy sat and waited, finding a new level of slowness that even the buzzing flies seemed to stop to admire. He pictured his sister racing along the farm tracks, weaving between potholes, the wind loud in her ears. He tried not to think about it, distracting himself with the knowledge that she would soon be back, and then it wouldn't be long before the strange thing happened again.

Usually he heard her before he saw her, the faint clattering of the mudguards signalling her return. Then there she was, never going as fast as he'd imagined, her legs making their slow circuits as she pedalled. Placing the bike back against the fence, she would speak one last time to Spider – she's saying thank you, Billy thought, she was always saying thank you – then gather up her egg and leave, all thoughts of following her younger brother apparently forgotten. For a minute or two Spider would stay in the run (Billy only saw it the first time because he was himself slow to leave, distracted by some ants that were taking a shortcut over his foot), but then out he would come, walking round to where the bike leant. Bending over, he lowered his head until his nose was touching the bike's saddle. And then, with Billy alert again as he watched, he started taking deep breaths. One slow inhalation followed another, his chest swelling as he breathed in through his nose, pausing now and then to exhale through his mouth and look quietly about.

The joint of meat sat on the table before them. The old man had cooked it days ago, and every evening since they'd whittled away at it. Today they'd finally stripped the bone bare. Using the handle of a teaspoon, the old man dug out as much of the marrow as he could. He passed it to Billy.

'It's good for you,' he said, and without a moment's hesitation Billy put it in his mouth. 'That's it,' said the old man, 'that's the way.'

Grace was trying to shift the image of Easter's penis from her mind. So long and thick, with dark bits encrusted around the tip. The memory made her queasy. It was so big, the size of her arm, maybe longer, and maybe thicker too. The only ones she'd seen before were Michael's and Billy's. Michael's once, briefly, coming out of the bathroom early one Saturday morning, when he must have thought she was still asleep (he had reacted instantly, his hands darting down to cover himself), and Billy's a few times when he was younger. She'd seen it in Devon too; he'd been changing with his back to her in their room when he got a foot stuck and fell over, exposing himself. His was like a bald worm, about a third of the size of Michael's. But both had been soft dangling things, and nothing like the rigid, feet-long branch she had seen earlier. She put down her knife and fork, her appetite gone.

'Easter and Jenny,' she said. 'They're not really related, are they?'

The old man blinked at her and then returned to his plate. She was about to ask again when he spoke. 'Mother and son, like I told you. Easter day, nineteen—'

'No,' she said, shaking her head, 'they can't be.' She paused. 'Not after what I saw them doing.'

The old man peered up at her again through his glasses. 'Oh,' he said. 'I see. I suppose you're about to tell me that it's not right, that it's unnatural or some such.'

'But it *is* unnatural.'

'For who?'

'What were they doing?' said Billy next to her.

'It's just not natural for a mother and a son to want to do that.'

'Maybe not to your way of thinking. But the fact is they do it, so you can't hardly say it's unnatural.' His shoulders rose and fell. 'It is what it is. All they know are their urges. Though I'll admit he does look to enjoy more than she does, but that's most likely her age as much as anything.'

'What were they *doing*?' said Billy again.

'Nothing,' said Grace, hardly believing what she was hearing. 'They weren't doing anything.'

She fell silent. But she couldn't shake the shock of it: the struggle and the aggression, the raw physicality of it all. It had almost been as if they were fighting. She'd seen animals having sex like that before on television, but it was different when you were standing next to them, and when you knew it was a mother and her son you were watching. *A mother and her son.* She looked over at the old man, at the slow working of his jaw as he ate. He doesn't care, she thought. He watches them do it but he doesn't care.

She tried to eat some more, to think of something else, but still it stayed. She knew all about sex, of course she did, but seen up close it was impossible to imagine it being anything but painful. She'd explored inside herself with her fingers, but not for pleasure; the pleasure was all on the outside. Those times when she touched herself, it didn't occur to her that she might want something in there as well.

Billy was talking. 'That's over fifty now,' she heard him say, 'and I don't know how many rats. I was counting but then I threw some away and I forgot what number I was on. It's a lot, but not as many as the coloureds.'

'Good,' said the old man, nodding without glancing up. 'That's good.'

'Billy, don't say that,' said Grace.

'Don't say what?'

'Just don't call them that. It's not a nice word.'

He frowned at her. 'But that's what they are. They're not white so they're coloured, and they're the ones I shoot.'

Grace knew about the doves and what Billy was doing to them. The old man had a word for it – 'culling', he called it – and when she'd first heard it she'd assumed it was his accent, that he meant 'killing'. But now she'd heard it enough times to know it was a different word, even if as far as she could tell it meant the same thing. Each time she saw a collection of feathers around the barns she knew it was where something had died, where Billy had ended a life. She remembered picking the feathers from his T-shirt the day Liz had come. His capacity for killing was amazing to her, and it made her angry. Sitting there, she thought again of the emptiness of the farm, of the two donkeys and the dried hoof marks on the track beyond. Her anger grew; it seemed to rise in her with every thought. There were the donkeys and the old man's reaction, and the transformation of her little brother into a killer of small animals. He'd accepted the idea so easily, that the colour of something's feathers could determine whether it lived or died. There too – always there – was her anger at what had happened on the beach, and at the strange life they were now forced to live, to protect even, in case Liz should return and decide to split them up. She looked at the old man opposite her, and remembered what he'd said when the fox died about Lynn not liking him. As she looked at him, Grace felt she understood why. She kept looking, and in his face all her unhappiness suddenly found a focus.

'No wonder we never came here before.' Her voice sounded shaky, and she realised she was close to tears. The old man didn't look up, but his chewing ceased. 'It's horrible,' she said, unable to stop now she'd started, 'there's nothing but rats and doves, and now you've got Billy killing them too.' Her words reverberated around the walls of the kitchen. 'There's not even cows here any more. Just their hoof marks out there, dried into the track. It's horrible,' she said again, louder now, 'horrible and empty, and full of death. I wish we'd never come here.'

She stopped. The kitchen seemed quieter than before. Opposite her she saw a deep breath move through the old man, as a wind might rise to fill a sail before dying away again. When it had passed he looked straight at her.

'Where did the cows go?' said Billy.

The old man laid down his knife and fork, and sat back in his chair. Grace saw the sadness in his face. As she looked, she wondered if in fact it hadn't always been there, only now there was no mistaking it.

For a long time no one said anything. Eventually it was Billy's patience that failed him.

'The *cows*,' he said. 'Where did they go?'

'Nowhere,' said the old man. His voice was thicker than usual, and instead of looking at Grace or Billy he stared past them. Behind his glasses his eyes looked very small. 'They didn't go anywhere. They're still here, every last one of them. The milking herd, the heifers, the bull – all of them.' Still he

144

stared past them. 'The dry cows and the calves, some as young as a few days, some with their mothers' tongues still on them. No,' he said, shaking his head, 'they didn't go anywhere. Didn't have a choice; they weren't allowed to leave. It was all the rest of it that went. Those others, they took it with them. In their vans and their Land Rovers, in the pockets of their coats.' Gradually he slowed. His arms lay heavily on the table in front of him. 'All of it. They took it all with them, as surely as the ocean took your mother.'

It was the last he would say all evening. Grace and Billy cleared the table in silence, this the first thing they'd done together since Liz's visit. The old man was still sitting there when the time came for them to go to bed. Before climbing the stairs, Billy picked Jackson up and placed him on his lap. Slowly those great arms came alive again, moving from the table to hold him.

Grace lay awake late into the night. Holding her breath, she heard Billy's next to her, coming slowly and regularly as he slept. She wondered if the old man was asleep downstairs; she pictured his and Jackson's chests rising and falling to the same rhythm, their hair equally white in the darkness.

The bedsprings creaked as she turned onto her side. She remembered her outburst, and with it came a sense of her own selfishness. Lynn hadn't just been their mother; she'd been the old man's daughter, too. She'd been his daughter for longer than she and Billy had been alive. As she lay there she did her best to make sense of what the old man had said about the cows and those others taking the rest away, in their vans and in their pockets. Above all, she felt bad for what she'd said about wishing they'd never come here.

It was a long time before the first hints of sleep began to creep into her. Before she finally drifted off, one last thought occurred to her: in the old days I always fell asleep thinking about tomorrow; now I only think about the day that's gone.

The old man stepped into the moonlight. It was brighter outside than in the kitchen, and he could see Jackson quite clearly as he trotted ahead into the grass. The air was damp, but only in the way that suggests another hot day to come.

It pained him to remember what the girl had said. Perhaps she was right, perhaps they shouldn't have come after all. He remembered his surprise when the red-haired woman had told him how keen his grandchildren were to come and live with him. How they'd both said how much they loved the farm and felt it was what their mother would have wanted. In the days that followed he'd repeated those same words to himself. *What their mother would have wanted*. However often he said it, he couldn't bring himself to believe that it was true.

Jackson returned, and together they stepped back inside. The old man walked along the corridor to the sitting room. The girl's words went with him. If her face reminded him of Lynn, then so did her anger. Knowing this added to his sadness, and as he settled into his chair he was only grateful that Margaret wasn't there to see it.

As he breathed out he remembered the effort of burying the fox cub, how the sweat had run off him as he worked in the moonlight, and how when he was finished some of his face had felt numb. He looked around the room, at the familiar objects he could see now in the moonlight that came in through the window. Only in here was he beyond the emptiness of the farm; only in here did he have a sense of how things had been before. This room, the only place on the farm untouched by change.

His heavy shoulders sagged. The dreams came quickly; they had to, for he didn't sleep for long. At first he was alone, walking out to the lower meadow to bring in the herd for the evening milk. The afternoon was hot, the sky clear, and when he reached the field he found several of the herd up by the gate, gathered in the shade of the chestnut tree. Leaving the gate open behind him he struck out across the field, heading towards the boundary hedge where he knew number 304 would be. She was a nuisance; the only way to shift her was from behind. Suddenly Jackson was there, only younger, rushing ahead of him through the grass.

He stopped and bent down, testing with his fingers. In the prolonged heat the grass had lost some of its lushness, but the ground wasn't hard like it was around the rest of the farm and he wasn't worried. Because of the narrow band of water that ran between steep banks over to his right, there was enough food to last them a while yet. Although the stream was only a yard or two wide, and a foot deep, without it the farm would be a different place. Constantly watering the meadows it flowed between, it kept his cows in grass long after the other farms' pastures had dried up. Here and there the banks had caved in under their hooves where they crossed. Wide pools marked the spots, the water slow and deep.

The herd was on the move now. Already the first animals were on the track back to the farm, ambling their way along the familiar route. In the field the old man ran his eye over the cows as they passed him. One was limping, and he made a note of her number. He saw the flies that lined their eyes like creatures at a waterhole. He reached number 304. 'Come on,' he said. She looked up at him, her mouth working from side to side as she ate. She didn't move. 'You're an old cow and you don't yield much milk,' he said, moving behind her, 'so if I were you I'd get on with it, before I ask Fred the Dead to call round.' He put a hand on her rump and pushed. She resisted, leaning back against him. 'Go *on*,' he said, pushing with all his strength. Again she resisted. I might as well try and push over a tree, he thought to himself, and he raised his hand and brought it back down hard against her. Slowly, begrudgingly, she began to walk.

He followed her back towards the gate. Her tail swished to and fro. One of her hooves landed in a cowpat, opening it up. The flies that were on it took to the air, buzzing madly around before settling again. Now, instead of Jackson, the boy was beside him. He was wearing shorts and rubber boots that were too big for him; they made a hollow sound against his calves as he walked. He carried a hazel stick with several leaves still sprouting from its top. Mostly he only walked with it, but now and again, when the old cow in front slowed up and lowered her head to graze, he swung the thin end forward and gently tapped her on the hocks, keeping her on the move. Reluctantly she loped on. The boy hurried to keep up, his short legs and the boots and the long grass hindering his progress. The old man strolled along next to him, enjoying the sun on his back and the hum of the meadow that rose to meet him, the smells of newly grazed grass and fresh manure proof of the cycle in motion. It lay all around like an invisible mist; he could feel it on his face and in his lungs, and each living thing there shared in it. It was like all the spring days he had ever known combined. It was, he thought, the smell of life itself.

Most of the herd were well ahead of them by the time they reached the track. Dust idled in the air. It smelt different here, and even in the dream the old man felt his regret as he left the meadow behind him. The verges were churned up, the hogweed and the cow parsley trampled where the cows had tried to avoid the harder ground of the track. There flints and other stones lay in wait for them, their sharp edges half exposed by the cows' own hooves. Each day the animals stuck to the softest ground they could find, and each day more stones were uncovered. Number 304 did likewise now, walking tight up against the hedge, brushing against the hawthorn. Here and there grew oak trees; in places black and white hairs were caught up in the roughness of their bark, and in other areas their trunks were rubbed smooth.

The old man heard the tell-tale sound of hoof on stone come from the cow in front. When he came to any large flints he kicked them into the hedge. Opposite him the boy tried to do the same, but the oversized boots made him stumble. He bent down and picked them up with both hands, lobbing them as best he could out of the way. In his enthusiasm he forgot about the hazel stick, leaving it lying on the track behind them.

They were nearing the farm when things started to change. Most of the herd was up ahead in the holding yard, but three or four hung back, moving so slowly that even number 304 caught up and passed them. The old man checked their numbers. The cow he'd seen limping in the meadow was among them, but now three more were sore on their feet.

He looked around for the boy, finally spotting his boots beneath one of the cows. When the animal shifted he realised something was different. He looked closer. It looked like the boy – his eyes were right, his ears were right – but it wasn't. It was Lynn. She was the same age as the boy had been, and in the dream the old man realised that he too was younger.

150

Then came the sound of a vehicle. A Land Rover pulled into the farmyard and came to a standstill. The engine died. For a time nothing happened, and the old man looked back at Lynn. She returned his gaze without expression, as if his surprise was unfounded, as if it had been her all along. Strings of saliva hung down from the mouth of the cow next to her. He watched it pool in the dust. In the yard the Land Rover door opened, and a man stepped out. Here the dream started to break up, the different moments no longer flowing so smoothly together. Now there were three other vehicles parked beside the Land Rover. Their doors were also open, and more men were hunched over, looking for things concealed inside. Then they were standing around in a group, all of them wearing the same things: the boots, the overalls, the jackets. The next time the old man looked – the final time, before Jackson's struggles woke him – all he could see was black smoke hanging heavily over the farm.

PART THREE

9

Billy watched and waited. The sun was up now, but still he waited. The sound of the cockerel crowing came again from the chicken run. A young rat scurried across the yard, disappearing into the old milking parlour through a drainpipe. He watched it go, and inside the parlour the woodpigeon and her two half-grown chicks watched it arrive.

He shivered. The dawn chill lingered around the barn and other buildings, clinging to the brick and stone like a fledgling to the nest. He shivered again, and drew his knees up closer into himself. Had he worn a watch he might have watched the seconds tick by, counting off the minutes before moving. But recently he'd developed his own sense of the right moment. It always came if you were patient; the trick was recognising it when it did.

Another rat caught his eye as it crossed the yard below him. It was a good hiding place: from here he could see and not be seen. Grace would never come up here because of the smell. Beneath him, under black plastic that was soft to walk on and warm to the touch, was the biggest pile of rotting grass he'd ever seen. He knew it was grass because he'd cut a hole and had a look. It was damp in there, and along with the smell came a gush of sickly heat.

Dozens of old tyres of different sizes lay over the plastic, weighing it down, and it was inside the largest of these – a tractor tyre that sat at the very summit like a screw-top lid – that he'd chosen to hide. Nearly six feet across and a third as deep, it provided enough space for him and anything else he cared to bring along. The airgun lay inside the rubber rim, next to the tin of WASPS. There too was a knife he'd found in one of the sheds, its point buried in a wooden workbench. The tip had gleamed silver when he pulled it out, bright and brilliant next to the rest of the rusty blade.

It was time. Whether it was a change in the light or the taste of the air he couldn't say, but he knew that Spider would soon be here on his bicycle. He'd given the chickens as long as he dared. He paused on his haunches before climbing out, and saw how the rubber was scored with nicks and deeper tears, the huge tread worn down nearly flat. He made his way over the heap, stepping from tyre to tyre, feeling the stiffness start to leave his legs. Since cutting the hole he didn't like to walk directly on the plastic in case he hit a weak spot and it opened up and swallowed his foot. His eyes worked ahead of each step, mapping his route. The whole thing was a kind of jigsaw: now and then he'd see a tyre that triggered the memory of one like it he'd seen somewhere else. But instead of wanting to reorganise them, to group them up and complete the puzzle, he liked the randomness of it all. He'd never understood why people did jigsaws; the urge to organise was alien to him. To begin with a jumble of pieces that you then put in order was so much less appealing than to take the perfect picture and mix it up – as his teachers and fellow pupils at Maddox Primary had often discovered to their cost.

He reached the drop-off. Before starting the climb down he paused once more to look about. The yard was quiet, the farmhouse peaceful. The sun was getting stronger, but still there was no sign of Spider. The cockerel crowed again, and this time Billy turned and watched it stretch its whole body upwards, as if being straighter eased the passage of the sound. I wonder why it does it, he thought. I wonder why it shouts like that when all the others cluck quietly about.

Suddenly something sprang out from one of the tyres close to him and streaked away over the heap, going the opposite way from him and disappearing over the edge. It was a fox. He'd seen one before skulking around the perimeter of the farm, but he'd had no idea they could move that fast.

He looked inside the tyre. The plastic in the centre was

polished clean from where the animal had been lying. Hairs were stuck all around the rim, and there were feathers too. He reached down and picked one up; holding it between his finger and thumb he examined it. A dove feather. There were several of them, and he got down on his hands and knees and searched the tyre properly. Hidden in the nearside rim was a dove wing; next to it lay a thin bone, clean and white. He held it up, turning it at different angles as he tried to work out which part of the bird it had been. There was a hole in it that could, he thought, have been made by a WASP. It was certainly the right size. He imagined the fox swimming out into the muck hole and grabbing one of the bodies with its mouth. It must have been starving to do that. He threw the bone back into the tyre.

It felt good to be back on firm ground. It was still damp from the night, and his soles left their mark behind him as he walked. He would have to be quick: just as he'd learnt to detect when the time was right, he had a sharp sense of when the moment had passed.

The chickens raised their heads as he approached. They appeared unsure if they should be wary of this small human, or hopeful that he was bringing them something to eat. Perhaps somewhere in their tiny brains they held a memory of his visit the previous morning when he hadn't brought them anything. As he hurried closer they decided on the former; by the time he opened the gate most of them were grouped up against the far side of the enclosure. He went straight to the wooden shed on wheels, startling a big brown hen that hadn't seen him coming. Caught in no man's land, it sidestepped back and forth before bolting past him.

With his hand on the shed door he closed his eyes and hoped that this time it would be different. The previous morning, standing in the shed with the chickens squawking their surprise and annoyance at being disturbed at such an early hour, he'd found nothing. He'd searched again, feeling with his hand in the hay. Three times his fingers stumbled blindly into soft little piles of droppings, but still he searched. And then it had happened: he'd touched something hard and oval. It's an egg, he said under his breath: *it's an egg, it's an egg, it's an egg.* As his fingers curled around it he saw in his mind the small bent saucepan sitting on the stove. It would still be half full of water from when it was last used. He'd look for some bread (partly because of the apparently magical way it sometimes appeared, and partly because it was the nicer thing to believe, he never lost hope that there would be bread) while the water warmed. There was still some butter left – that much was certain. He would leave the egg in for the time it took to boil, and then a bit longer after that. He could almost taste the yolk as it thickened on his tongue.

He'd held the egg up in front of him. Needles of light threaded their way into the shed through gaps and holes in the wooden walls; tiny particles from the hay passed through them like drifting plankton. Looking to see if it was a brown one or a blue one he saw it was neither. Even in the gloom its surface gleamed white. It was strangely heavy, and while half a minute ago this had pleased him, now it worried him. He ran his thumb over the shiny surface, squinting to see in the half-light. Instead of the smoothness he'd expected, he felt tiny chips and marks. His thumb passed over one end. It couldn't be … but it was. A hole, perfectly circular, and into which his thumb slotted easily. His first thought was that it had hatched, that a chick had somehow managed to make a neat opening and burrow its way out. But then why still so heavy?

He'd carried it outside and turned it over in his hands, hardly believing what he was seeing. It was an egg all right, but a fake one. It was made of the same sort of thing as cups and plates. Stains marked the areas where the glaze had chipped off, and if it hadn't been for his hunger he might have found something pleasing about the strange object he held in his hands. Most likely he would have put it in his pocket and spent the rest of the day taking it out for another look, turning it over and over until much of the staining was rubbed off. Even as he looked at it, a part of Billy knew this about himself: the desire to keep and treasure was still there.

The chickens had stood about watching him from a distance, confused by the morning's disturbances. Only the cockerel appeared unworried, chasing after a little black and gold hen, pursuing her through the dust. Billy saw none of it. He'd thrown the egg down as hard as he could; it thudded into the ground, lying half submerged before him. He'd picked it up again and looked around. His eyes settled on the area of concrete beyond the run that marked the beginning of the farmyard. A second later the china egg was soaring into the air above it. A further second and the sound of its collapse reached him.

He opened his eyes. Today would be different: the extra time he'd given the chickens to lay would surely help. Opening the shed door he stepped inside. The sun was higher than the previous morning and more light leaked in, but tucked away in the recesses the laying troughs remained shrouded in darkness. His fingers moved carefully through the hay as he searched. After a while his hand landed on something feathery, and he sprang back when it was met with a sharp peck. He held his hand up to one of the shafts of light. There was no blood, but the skin by one of his knuckles was marked white.

The worst part of the previous day hadn't been finding the fake egg: it was later on, when he saw Spider giving Grace a real one. He'd been up in the tyre when his sister came ambling up the farmyard. The usual thing had happened: Spider saw her and stopped what he was doing, and rushed towards the gate. But then he'd realised she was coming to him. After talking for a time he'd disappeared into the hen-house. There aren't any in there, Spiderman, Billy had said to himself. The thought had pleased him: if he had to live on vegetables then so should she. But then there he was, back out in the sunlight, egg in hand and shifting from foot to foot.

Billy glanced around the inside of the hen-house. He had an idea. Snapping off a side branch from one of the roosting poles he prodded about in the darkness. When he felt two sharp taps he pushed harder, until the chicken appeared in a flurry of feathers and rushed outside, squawking loudly as it joined the others. He reached in to where it had been. Feeling with his fingers he found the turn of hay the chicken had shaped about itself. He found the hollow within it. But inside the hollow there was only a lingering warmth.

Outside, Billy took deep breaths. He couldn't understand it. He looked about, and then got down on his hands and knees and peered beneath the hen-house. There were stray feathers, flints, old bits of wood. But then something else caught his eye. He circled around to the other side; there on the ground before him, hidden between the hen-house and the fence, was a little wire run. It was pushed up against a coop. A brick weighed down a piece of wood that served as a roof.

He pushed off the brick and lifted the board. A chicken blinked up at him. It started to puff out its plumage, spreading its wings so that it filled the space. He was still holding the stick from before, and he reached down and began to shoehorn the bird off its nest. It was more difficult than it looked – the bird was surprisingly heavy – and twice when he thought he'd managed it the chicken rolled back into place. Both times he glimpsed the tell-tale flash of blue beneath. Instead of trying to peck him, this chicken's defence seemed to be to do nothing, to go limp, and when for a third time it slid back over the eggs his patience ran out. He drove the stick down harder until he felt the soft belly of the bird, and with a sudden jerk he up-ended it, wedging it against one side of the coop. And there, neatly laid out before him, except for a couple that had rolled out with the chicken, was his prize.

He took all of them, gathering them up into the upturned hem of his T-shirt. The chicken watched without moving, and he wondered briefly if he'd hurt it. 'It's your fault,' he said aloud to it, 'you should've moved.' Even as he replaced the board and brick it stayed hunched to one side of the nest.

Letting himself out through the gate he hurried back across the concrete towards the shade and safety of the buildings. It's not stealing, he said to himself. It can't be stealing: you can't steal from a chicken. But still the feeling that he'd done something wrong remained. He must hide them. His thoughts turned immediately to the tyre, but just as quickly he decided against it, seeing himself falling on the upward climb, the eggs crushing into an inedible mess. The thought of it made him laugh, and he said to himself, aloud this time, 'I want them *in* my stomach, not *over* it.'

He hurried on towards the farmhouse. Grace would still be in bed, and the old man would be in the little room at the end of the corridor. His excitement rose as he imagined taking him an egg, the top already lifted off. He hadn't eaten for days – maybe he should take him two. He could already picture the way he would slowly sit up in his chair and spoon out the yolk, savouring each mouthful, his tongue working around his mouth the way it did. When he'd finished the first one Billy would bring him the second, and sitting down he'd eat his own there next to him. When the old man was done, most likely he'd go back to sleep. The best thing about it was that Grace would never know. Even if she came downstairs while they were eating, she'd walk right past the door.

A rattling noise came from up ahead. He was only a short distance from the farmhouse – he'd be there in less than a minute – but something in him stalled, and he stood rooted to the spot. The rattling came closer, and then there was Spider, his head and eyes perched over the handlebars of the bicycle while his sinewy legs worked away below. Billy's grip on his T-shirt tightened, his other hand curling around in front of him, cradling his load like a pregnant woman. Spider came straight at him, passing by within a couple of feet. With his chin tucked in, Billy half turned away from him, shielding his face and front as best he could from the quick little eyes that darted over him. There was a pause in the pedalling, their creaking circuit falling silent, and he held his breath. He heard the tyres biting into the stone and dust. Staying perfectly still, he waited. The creaking started again, continuing on up the yard behind him, growing quieter by the second. He breathed out and dared to turn around.

Spider was crossing the concrete area; in a short time he'd be at the chicken run. Beneath him Billy's legs came alive again, and he ran the rest of the way as fast as he could, wanting only to be out of reach of those quick eyes.

The farmhouse was as silent as he'd left it. Standing on the lino in the kitchen he looked around for a suitable hiding place. He turned back into the hallway. Kneeling down by the door he pulled one of the rubber boots closer until it stood beside him. The sole and foot were covered in what must have once been mud; lumps of it dropped off at the disturbance and crumbled on the floor. Handing the eggs out one by one he placed them inside the boot, his arm disappearing up to the shoulder. When he had four left he replaced the boot and stood back to see if anyone might notice. No, he decided, his hands twitching at his sides with satisfaction, no one would ever guess.

He carried the remaining four through to the kitchen. The bent saucepan was on the stove just as he'd imagined it. Jackson appeared, and Billy knelt and stroked him, feeling the raised ridge of his backbone. 'Are you hungry?' he said, seeing the way the terrier raised his nose towards the stove, smelling the eggs. Jackson looked up at him and Billy scratched him behind his broken ear. 'Okay,' he said, and fetching another egg from the boot he added it to the water.

Not long afterwards Billy was still in the kitchen. He stood over the sink, staring down at the four remaining eggs.

Boiled clean, their blue shells looked fresh. He picked one up. Cracking it against the porcelain, he started to peel it. He stopped halfway and put it with the first one that already sat on the counter next to him. He picked up another, which he also cracked and half peeled, and another, and then another, until all five sat before him, each now nothing more than a watery ball of blood and feather and beak, their unborn, unseeing eyes barely discernible through the mess.

Grace stirred. Something had woken her: a noise, a slammed door perhaps. She didn't need to turn over and look to know that he was gone again. She lay there, unmoving, her eyes closed as she listened. She could tell from the birds outside that it was early: the newness of the day still clung to their song. Half awake, she pictured them singing on their perches, their eyes bright and their beaks wide, until the sun rose and moved overhead, scorching them into submission. Perhaps the air gets too dry, she thought sleepily, and their song gets stuck in their throats. Maybe that's it.

Her stomach rumbled under the sheet. In another few hours I'll go and see Spider, she promised herself, and this time I'll try to get as many eggs as I can. She thought of his bicycle leaning against the wire. She remembered freewheeling down the farm drive and then pedalling along the lane. Field had followed field, each as identical as the last. She'd begun to wonder if fields were all that was left in the world. When she came to a fork in the road, the muscles in her legs ablaze from the effort, there'd been no signpost, no clue as to which way the village was. She even began to question whether the old man had really said there was a village, or if she'd simply imagined it. Perhaps the town was all there was. Remembered afresh, the cobbled square with its rows of shops had seemed a distant and hostile place. She'd cycled on and on, seeing not another soul, losing her sense of time and distance in the unchanging landscape. At last she'd found something, an old postbox set in brick, and partially obscured by ivy. Pulling the strings of leaves to one side she'd tried to read the collection notice, but water had got in and fogged up the glass. And then the fear had come: that she might not find her way back to the farm; that she might get a puncture; that Spider might be angered by her extended absence; and, worst of all, that because of this anger, her supply of eggs might cease.

She lay still, waiting to hear anything else. Silence. The sleepiness was slowly leaving her; she imagined it as an invisible film covering her like dew, which, as the day warmed, dried and evaporated like everything else. She wondered how the old man managed to keep his own film so tightly wrapped about him. Most days it never left him completely, and recently it didn't seem to at all.

She sat up. Her legs were a deeper colour than they'd ever been before, and she hardly recognised herself. A few minutes later, standing naked in the bathroom, she caught sight of herself in the mirror, seeing the areas of white that usually lay hidden beneath her shorts and T-shirt. They're the only parts of me that are unchanged, she thought to herself, they're the only bits that haven't been affected by what happened on the beach. She found comfort in knowing this, and took pleasure in the idea of preserving these reminders of the girl she had once been. Perhaps in this way some of her happier self might be kept alive too.

More and more she found herself thinking like this. Where once her instinct had been to look forwards, nowadays she found it easier to stay within the confines of her memory. There was a certainty and a safety about the past: it was fixed, there were no surprises. However hard she tried to picture the future it was always blank, and it frightened her. Because of this she began to seek out the familiar wherever she could. One afternoon, feeling too fidgety to sunbathe, she'd walked out to the wind turbines. She'd hoped that by simply standing beneath them she might regain some of the optimism she'd felt before, with Mr Beazley and the rest of her class. By the time she got there she was tired and hot, and her flip-flops bit into her from the long trudge along the farm tracks. The turbines stood in a group, the ground around them so thick with poppies and nettles that she could only look from a distance. They were smaller than she'd expected; their masts were cracked and discoloured, and above her their blades were still. She'd stayed only a minute, with flies mobbing her face as they sought her sweat, before turning back.

Tied up among this sense of preservation were her parents; the thing that frightened her most was forgetting them. Sometimes she said their names aloud, in the hope that it would help her remember them better. One morning in bed she tried something else, tentatively trying the words out. 'Mum and Dad,' she said under her breath. She waited, and then said it again. 'Mum ... Dad.' But she felt nothing. The words sounded foreign, like they belonged to someone else.

Instead she concentrated on remembering how they'd talked and smiled and laughed. Above all she tried to remember their touch, particularly the hugs, of celebration and of comfort. She could only conjure a vague sense of how they'd felt, and she worried that she was beginning to forget these too. There were moments in the farmhouse when Billy passed within a foot or two of her that she was overcome with a desire to hold him, to feel his warmth against her own the way she had that first night. One evening she tried it, reaching out and pulling him to her, but he went so stiff she quickly let go again. She tried to make a joke of it, but all he did was look at her, his sombre expression unchanged. How has it come to this? she'd wondered to herself afterwards as they lay in their beds with the light out, not five feet from each other. How can I have lost him so completely in so short a space of time? But then she thought of Lynn and Michael. If she'd learnt anything it was that nothing was safe, least of all those things that were dearest to you. It could all be taken away at any moment.

She dressed and went downstairs. She opened the door. It was dead still: not even the tips of the long grass moved. She wondered again what had woken her. Perhaps it hadn't been a door at all, she thought, perhaps it was something else. In the kitchen she found Jackson; he looked up at her as she entered, before moving stiffly past her into the corridor, his back feet hardly leaving the ground as he walked. The lino where he'd been standing was wet, the surface shiny. When she looked closer, she saw fragments of shell.

She stood up, confused. These days she was the only person who brought eggs into the house, and the one Spider had given her yesterday she'd already eaten. She looked about. The table was as she'd left it, but the sink had been used. She checked the saucepan on the stove. The water was hot.

She hurried out of the kitchen and along the corridor. She wasn't sure what she expected, but all she found was the old man, asleep with Jackson at his feet, his hands interlocked over his stomach which rose and fell with the same deep regularity. The only other sound came from the few flies that buzzed at the window. She stood in the doorway, not understanding. She looked at Jackson's swollen stomach and the contented way he rearranged his back legs on the carpet as he prepared to sleep. How can this be? she thought, remembering the hot saucepan. *How can this be?*

She looked again at the old man as he slept. He'd stopped shaving. At first his face had looked as if it had been dusted with flour, but then as the days passed his beard had grown, giving the impression of a crop he was tending from within. He hadn't lost weight like she and Billy had, yet he'd refused to eat anything for days. Instead he sat in that chair, sometimes awake, more often asleep, never saying a word. No longer did she hear his laborious climb up the stairs to the bathroom, nor did she find the usual ring of scum around the sink.

She returned to the kitchen and cut herself some bread. She hoped the old man would leave his chair soon to bake some more. She thought of the vegetable patch, and felt grateful for the rows of greenery that had fed Billy and her since the meat had run out. Sometimes she went over the areas they'd already dug, checking for anything they might have missed. But the soil was empty, and without the shade afforded it by the plant above, the ground soon dried out and cracked, the same as everywhere else.

She spooned some honey onto the bread, and then relished the sweetness as she chewed. Often she went and stood by the beehive, watching the bees come and go, the black and brown of their bodies changing as they moved from light to shade and back again. She soon came to admire them, for their labour and the hours they kept; always hard at work by the time she was up, they'd be safely inside as dusk fell. She imagined them arranged in neat rows like an army, or instead as a writhing, humming ball that grew slowly quieter as they slept. She tried to picture the honey inside but couldn't. Was it collected in a mound at the centre of the hive? Or were there small pools of it, dotted all around? She didn't know. Once she came too close: instantly the number of bees outside the hive doubled, the noise from them unmistakably louder. Quickly retreating, she'd watched from the paddock fence as they calmed.

It was spring, and the old man was about to see his first swallow of the year. Having made a final check of the fencing, he walked back towards the farm buildings. He was pleased: none of the posts had needed replacing. He hitched at his trousers as he went, his back pocket weighed down with a hammer and a handful of staples. At last the sun had some heat to it, and he slowed to enjoy it. There was a hatch of flies, and from somewhere close by came the sound of a chaffinch. There had been warm days already, but the heavy, squally showers of the early part of the week had persuaded him to wait. But this morning, from the very first moment he stepped outside, he'd known. It was as if the year had shed its old skin, revealing a newness beneath. This was what he'd been waiting for. For the milking herd, today would mark the end of winter: today they were going back out to pasture.

He was on the concrete of the holding yard when the swallow passed overhead. Seeing it, he felt the relief he always did that they'd returned. With swallows came luck – the year they stayed away would be a bad one. He thought this out of habit, but it was something Margaret had believed, and to think it was to be reminded of her.

He was still thinking it when he entered the calf shed. Before he slid the bolt across, around twenty black and white heads appeared from the pens on either side, all of them turned his way and each one greeting his arrival with loud bleats. The metal gates and partitions rattled as they moved around. He walked between them, filling their buckets; now and then he felt the rasp of a tongue catch his shirt. 'You'll get yours too,' he'd say, or, 'Hold you hard, I'm now coming.' Gradually the shed grew quieter, the mouths that had shouted so noisily now immersed in milk.

When he reached the end he turned to watch them feed. Occasionally one of them paused, raising its head from the bucket, the whiskers over its nose draped in white. Having checked that they weren't missing out on any more feed that might be coming their way, their noses disappeared again, and the only noise came from the buckets as they tried to gain extra purchase.

The old man was thinking about swallows. It only took a glance to see how lucky he'd already been this year: twice the number of pens on the left side were occupied as on the right, and these were the heifer calves. He couldn't help but think it as he looked at them: not long from now, each one of those little things will weigh half a ton. If my luck holds, I might get twenty litres of milk a day out of each of them. He looked at the pens on the right, at the squarer foreheads visible over the buckets. They were the unlucky ones. Without udders to milk and wombs with which to reproduce, bull calves weren't worth the cost to feed them.

Back out in the sunshine he decided to check the route once more. Following the track he passed beneath a clump of stunted pines. He cast his eye over the wire fence. He did it casually, for he knew well enough that it was sound. Finally, with nothing left to delay him, with a wave he sent Spider to start them moving.

They were reluctant at first, as if the winter inside had made them forget all about the open sky and the fields that surrounded the farm. Slowly it dawned on them, their memories jolted, and they rushed on ahead. Passing the old man the first of them reached the grass. Instantly they turned into mad things that leapt and kicked. Others stood shoulder to shoulder and pawed the ground with their hooves; clumps of grass were uprooted; fresh soil was bared to the light. Occasionally one of them took completely to the air, and the old man felt the shudder through his feet when it landed again. It's as if they're trying to wake the earth, he thought as he watched them. It's as if now they've remembered they want to remind the rest of the world that spring's here. But he knew it was quieter than that, that all he was really watching were old friends being reunited after a long separation. Nowhere was this closeness more evident than when an animal dropped to its knees and rubbed its jaw against the ground, moving back and forth as it nuzzled the dirt, even taking some of it into its mouth and over its tongue. He shook his head as he watched: no matter what he fed them, still there was something that could only be got from the ground.

He looked around at them, seeing the way their coats shone, the black and white lit up by the sunshine. He saw their straight backs and the squareness of their hips, their bones clear to see as they shifted beneath their skins. Just when it looked as if they were beginning to calm, a fresh wave of excitement moved through the younger animals, and they were off once more. Gradually they spread out and, at less risk of being crushed now, the old man walked among them. They began to graze, their heads down, and the rip of grass came from all about. A deep satisfaction moved through him, and so foreign was this feeling of happiness that the old man nearly woke. When a short while later he did, it was to Grace's concerned face; for not only was the old man smiling in a way that she'd never seen before, there was also the sound of engines coming from the yard.

10

The dust swirled around the machines as they moved up the farmyard. From where she stood Grace caught glimpses of them, the flashes of colour coming at her as though through a rainstorm. The noise from their engines added to the effect, reverberating like thunder between the buildings; she felt dwarfed by the hugeness of it, shocked by such a sudden and violent break to the quiet that she'd grown accustomed to. Somewhere in among them was the old man, gun in hand. She wondered if he'd be run down in the confusion. But then, as they drew level with her, the machines came to a standstill, and together the noise and dust fell away.

There before them stood the old man. The rifle had appeared from nowhere; he'd moved so quickly that even

Jackson had been left in his wake. Now he trotted over to him, his hackles rising as he went.

For a time nothing happened, and Grace was able to run her eyes over the newcomers without interruption. The lead machine was bright yellow; it bore the letters JCB. Attached to it was a trailer, and on this sat a mud-splashed jeep. Next was a machine that reminded her of a bulldog: its front end was enormous, while the rest of its body tapered away. Its wheels reflected the imbalance, with two large followed by two small. Its shiny red flanks towered over everything. From somewhere – from books or television or a distant memory – she recognised it as a combine harvester. She saw the little glass cab perched high up, and there inside was a man. His arms were crossed, but when he saw her looking he uncrossed them and waved. It was a casual enough gesture, but it made her heart race, and she felt the heat at her cheeks. By the time she waved back the moment was gone.

The cab of the JCB opened and a man stepped out. He wore a set of green overalls and leather work boots.

'Morning to you,' said the man. He reached up and scratched his head. 'I believe we ... ' His words dried up under the old man's scrutiny. He looked as if he was about to speak again when the cab of the combine opened behind him. The man who'd waved at Grace stuck his head out.

'Come on, Frank,' he shouted at the overalled man. 'We'd have half a field in the tank by now if you'd stop your chat.' He paused, as if seeing the rifle for the first time. 'What's this? A stick-up? Well, give him your bloody necklace then, and whatever else he wants – as soon as that's done we can get the fuck on with it.'

The man called Frank winced as the words rang out over his head. 'Please,' he said, looking at the old man, his forehead beginning to shine under the sun. 'It's Mr Ambrose, isn't it?' The old man didn't reply, and Grace wondered if he'd heard him. 'Please, pay him no regard – he's keen to get on, that's all. We all are. You know me as Mayhew, from out Melton way. I believe I'm right in saying we've a contract for some barley with you.' The old man stood before him, silent and unmoving. 'Well,' he continued, 'truth is I know we do – I was here in the winter when we drilled it. I oversaw it. Been a hell of a heat this last little while and we're flat out getting it all in around and about, and now we've come to you.' He glanced again at the rifle and at Jackson, whose hackles still stood up along his back. 'If today's no good we can come back another time, only it'd seem a pity what with having all the kit here now, and the boys along to use it. If we leave it now that might be a little while before we can get back – and judging from the way that's looking that barley wants to come now. It's time. It's the same everywhere, it's been one of them years, that's all come early. The grain's so dry you give it another week and I'll warrant it'll start dropping where it stands. We've had two fires already this week – there's not a drop of moisture left in the ground. It's like tinder.'

He hesitated, and when he spoke again his voice was quieter, as if he didn't want those behind him to hear.

'I know you've had your troubles this past while – there's others around here who have too, and many more besides – and I'm sorry for you, really I am. I don't know much about keeping livestock, and I can't imagine how that must feel to have that happen, but arable I do know, and the long and the short of it is that crop's ready, and we'd be pleased to get it in for you.' He ran the back of his hand over his forehead, smearing a dry patch in the sweat.

The farmyard was silent once more. Ambrose, thought Grace. She knew her mother had been Lynn Ambrose before she was Lynn Hooper, but there was something strange about hearing the same name used for the old man. It made her think of the life her mother had lived before, one that must have resembled her own now.

'Mayhew,' said the old man at last. He said it quietly, more to himself than anyone else. He lowered the rifle and looked up. 'I appreciate your being here.' His rumbling voice was the same pitch as the idling engines, and his words folded into the noise. Either detecting the change in his voice or simply losing interest, Jackson looked about and then sat down and scratched himself behind one ear. The old man glanced down at his feet, and seemed surprised to find that he was only wearing socks. The man called Frank clenched his jaw while he waited.

'I'd best find you a map of the farm,' said the old man.

Frank shook his head. 'There's no need. We know where we're going.' The old man nodded his understanding. 'Only thing we might want is the key to any locked gates around the place. That way we can get on and get done and be out of your way just as soon as we can.'

'No,' said the old man, 'nothing's locked now. You can go where you like.'

'Much obliged,' said Frank quickly, as if the old man might change his mind. With a brief nod in Grace's direction he climbed back into the JCB. A jet of smoke shot out from the exhaust, and the old man and Jackson made their way back over to Grace. Together they watched the machines pass them. First the JCB, then the combine, then three tractors, two pulling high-sided trailers and the third a strange-looking humpbacked machine that Grace didn't recognise. The dust rose about them once more, and although Grace couldn't see them, she knew there must be more men driving each one.

The old man walked back to the farmhouse, leaving Grace standing there alone. She'd always imagined farm equipment to be dirty, as if it should in some way reflect the job it did. The old bits of machinery she'd seen lying around the farm seemed more appropriate than these wheeled giants that glinted in the sun. More unnatural creatures were hard to imagine; watching them was like watching tanks heading off to battle. Was that what farming was, a struggle between man and nature? The idea saddened her: with every day that passed it seemed her ideas about the countryside were being undone. She pictured Spider's chickens scratching about in their run and found herself wondering: was the wire there to protect them or to control them? Then she remembered the power of the waves that day, and the damage they'd done. Perhaps struggling against nature was part of being human, of being alive. Perhaps it had always been that way.

She stood there until the noise of the machines had retreated into the distance. She thought of the men inside the glass cabs and of the fields of crop that awaited them. Finally, she turned and walked back to the farmhouse.

The heat of the day settled over the farm. It found its way everywhere, leaching in under doors and over window-sills. There was no escape; the air itself vibrated with the energy. In the fields the contractors kept watch, half expecting it to spark and catch at any moment.

To the north a plume of dust rose high into the sky, tracking the progress of the combine below. The crop fell noiselessly before the serrated teeth, too heavy with grain to resist. The tractor drivers sat by in air-conditioned comfort, listening to radios and watching the chaff fall like ash over their cabs. Then the time would come, and the combine's shuddering arm would swing out and fill their trailers one by one. Taking turns, they made the run back to the farmyard. Their wheels were too wide for the tracks, and soon the grass edges were flattened down, the wild seeds spilling into the dirt. Now and then grains of barley joined them, finding their way through cracks in the trailers as they passed over the rough ground, leaving a thin trail of gold that marked the way back to the farmyard. Gradually the grain bins began to fill.

After each load the driver climbed the ladder and checked the level, knocking with his hand on the metal until hard gave way to hollow. Then it was back the way they'd come, their trailers bouncing emptily over the same bumps, racing to be ready for when the combine's great red belly was full again. By then more of the crop would have vanished, and they could take to the field, driving where earlier things only grew. The stubble cracked and prickled as they went; small birds flitted between the rows of straw; molehills were visible in the earth. Had the drivers stopped to look they would also have seen patches of flattened barley where an animal had laid down, or the collection of feathers where a pheasant had panicked and frozen, before being sucked inside and having the life threshed from it. They might even have seen the footprints in the tramlines, of foxes and of deer; and there among them, the tread of his trainers clear to see, those of a young boy.

11

Grace paced up and down, not knowing what to do. Outside dusk was falling, and still there was no sign of Billy. The old man too was gone from his chair. She wondered if he was back out there, blocking the contractors' path as he had earlier. Stepping outside she stood and listened. The sound of the machines moving back and forth, the pitch of their engines rising and falling, reached her on the evening air.

Back inside she took to pacing once more. Jackson appeared and followed her from room to room, even trailing upstairs after her, his paws sounding strange on the wooden steps. She decided to check the old man's bedroom. She edged the door open. It was empty. She stepped inside, casting about for any clues that he'd been in there. The stack of newspapers she'd found before caught her eye, and again she wondered why he'd kept them. She looked closer at the top copy. The paper was beginning to yellow; PREVENTION MEASURES NOT ENOUGH read the headline. Below it was a picture of some cows standing in a field. She lifted it up and looked at the one beneath. EXCLUSION ZONE WIDENS. She carried on, working her way through the pile until she came across one that held her attention. She read the single word over and over by the last of the light until the letters were just shapes on the page. DISEASE.

What the man called Frank had said to the old man returned to her. 'I know you've had your troubles this past while.' She'd assumed he'd been talking about Lynn. She remembered what the old man had said about the herd still being here, and how it was all the rest of it that had been taken from him. Finally, with a rush of guilt, she remembered her own words from that evening.

She found herself strangely incapable of moving. She knew well enough that she should do something, but sitting there in the half-light she felt detached from everything around her. It was as if she was the tiniest fleck of existence in the whole world. She wondered if Lynn had sat here once and felt the same thing. She imagined living like this for months, or years, the way the old man must have done. She glanced back at the stack of newspapers, at the top copies she'd disturbed in the otherwise neat pile. She listened. There, embroidered in the silence, was her and the old man's shared loss. His was a life unnoticed, one that went unobserved in all its detail. For him there was only the passing of each day. Perhaps this had frightened Lynn the same way it scared her now; perhaps that was why she'd so rarely mentioned her own time here.

Darkness fell. How long had she been sitting there? She didn't know. In the end it was the silence that moved her, for there too in it was Billy's absence. She went downstairs, and looking along the passageway towards the sitting room she found herself wishing that the old man had told her and Billy what had happened, had explained why the farm was the way it was.

Not knowing what else to do, she left the farmhouse and began to walk up the yard. The night air was cool. A thin layer of cloud had moved in over the sky. Behind it the moon was only dimly visible, a pale sickle robbed of its sharpness. As she came closer she made out the shape of the tractors in the glow of their own lights. The low purr of their engines reached her, and she heard voices. Two figures were standing behind one of the tractors, one of them leaning against a back wheel. She knew immediately from their shapes that neither of them were Billy or the old man. Walking close by, she felt grateful for the cover of darkness. For a time neither of them noticed her, and she was able to listen to their conversation.

'It wants a new bearing,' said one of them. From his voice she recognised Frank. 'I'll pick one up in the morning, and Jimmy can fit it before he starts.'

'Bastard thing'll only do it again,' said the other man.

'Hello, it's the young miss of the farm.'

Grace started, realising that they'd seen her. She smelt smoke, and saw that the other man held a cigarette in his hand.

'We're now finishing up for the night. That dew stayed off longer than what we'd hoped, and he's only now on his way back. A quick wash down and we'll be off home.' She could make out just enough to see that he was smiling at her. She stood where she was, not knowing what to say. 'Been a rare old heat today,' he continued, 'though I expect you've had the good sense to stay indoors. I've not known heat like it, not for a lot of years I haven't.'

'Hottest day yet,' said the other man.

'What's that? Today was? Is that right?'

The other man nodded in the gloom, drawing on his cigarette. 'They said so on the radio.' He turned away and spat on the ground.

'Well,' said Frank. 'Well,' he said again, 'there's a thing. If it gets any hotter we'll melt where we stand.'

They fell silent. Insects crowded the lights on the tractor; occasionally a big one landed on a bulb, blocking out some of the illumination and casting shadows much larger than itself. It stayed there, reluctant to relinquish its warm roost.

'Here on your holidays, are you?'

Grace shook her head, and then realised neither man had seen her do it. She changed her mind. 'Yes.'

'Your parents here with you?'

'No,' she said. 'It's just us.'

'Us?'

'My brother and me.'

'Oh your brother's here too, is he? That's nice. I expect Mr Ambrose is glad for the company.'

'I suppose,' she said.

'Another few weeks and it'll be back to school again, won't it? I'll bet you can't wait. See your friends again after the long summer.' He brought out a handkerchief and cleared his nose into it one nostril at a time. 'My son's the same,' he said when he was done, 'he's counting the days. You'd think we locked him up during the holidays. I say to him, "You can go to the village any time you want – no one's stopping you." I tell him he can come and work with me and earn himself a bit of pocket money, you know. "It won't be much," I say, "but you'll be learning a trade at the same time." But all he wants is to go up the town – and that means a half-hour drive and a lift from me or his mother.'

'And spending money,' said the other man without looking up.

'And spending money,' said Frank, nodding. 'He never can get enough of that.' He laughed a short little laugh.

'He's at that age, though, isn't he?' said the other man. From his voice Grace could tell he was older. 'They want all the nice things in life but they don't want to work for them.'

Frank took a deep breath, and Grace heard him let the air out of his nose. 'I suppose he is,' he said after a while. He looked at Grace through the darkness. 'How old's your brother?'

'He's only nine.'

'Well then, he's a way to go yet. Best tell your mum and dad to enjoy it while they can. I'll warrant you're not much trouble to them, though.' He paused as if expecting her to say something, but all she could think was *please stop talking about them, please*. 'Tell you what,' he went on, 'if he'd like a ride in the combine, your brother I mean, then you tell him to come and see me. We'll be making an early start tomorrow if the weather holds. We're not supposed to, mind, what with health and safety – and I dare say our insurers wouldn't be right keen on it—' next to him the older man snorted, '—but he might enjoy that. Never yet known a small boy able to resist a harvester; they'll watch them for hours if they can. Only,' he hesitated, 'only that's best if you check with Mr Ambrose first.'

There was a sound in the near distance. The men turned and looked towards it, and Grace followed their example. Coming along the track behind them, the majority of its bulk visible over the hedge, was the combine. It was covered in lights, and as it came closer the whining sound it made got louder. She remembered how she'd been confused by the lack of tractors on the farm, but now that there were some, along with this huge combine, they seemed out of place. All she'd seen for weeks was the crop blowing in the breeze. Were such vast and powerful machines really necessary to harvest it, when she could snap off a head of barley with her thumb and forefinger? And if they were so powerful, how was it that a thing like dew could stop them?

When Frank and the other man wandered over to the combine she took her chance and slipped away. The farmhouse was as dark and as empty as she'd left it. She tried to turn on a light but nothing happened. She ran her hands along the wall until she found another switch: still nothing. She made her way into the kitchen and felt about until she found a candle in one of the drawers. Unable to find any matches she thought to light it off the stove, but when she lifted the hob and tried, all the wick would do was glow. She could feel the heat rising onto her hand, and beneath her fingers the wax started to soften. She brought the tiny red ember before her face and blew on it, trying to coax it into life. Slowly it faded to nothing.

Her eyes adjusted to the gloom, aided by the shreds of moonlight that came in through the window. She found a box of matches on the window-sill, but as there seemed nothing left to do but go to bed she didn't bother with the candle. Not long afterwards, lying under the covers, she heard a vehicle leaving the yard. Now I'm truly alone, she thought. She imagined Frank and the other men talking together as they headed home, back to their wives and children. Again she wondered where Billy could be. Was it possible that he'd come back when she was talking to the men, and not finding anyone had left again? Maybe he was out there right now looking for her and the old man, or waiting until he saw a light come on in the farmhouse. Maybe I should be out there looking for him, she thought.

Pulling the covers back she went downstairs and opened the door and called his name. An owl screeched from somewhere over the fields. She shouted his name again, as loudly as she could. The owl was quiet. There was a snuffling sound behind her, and turning she saw Jackson's pale shape standing in the doorway, sniffing around the boots.

She turned back to the lawn. More cloud drifted in and covered the moon. She listened again, sensing all the birds and animals watching her, unseen out there in the blackness. She waited a while longer, but there was nothing.

That night the farm was restless. Like someone left too long to their own devices it seemed upset by the arrival of the contractors, by their noise and energy, and the work of their machines. Having had the peace of their day disrupted, the creatures of the sunless hours went about their business warily. If Grace had felt observed earlier, the old man would have been right to feel the same as he made his way back to the farmhouse. The eyes nearest him, however, saw nothing, for they belonged to the rabbit that swung from his right hand.

His grip on its back legs was weakening, and once he dropped it. The brown shape flopped onto the barley stubble, its limbs still loose and warm. He didn't notice for a few seconds, and when he did he turned and retraced his steps, casting about until he saw the white flash of its tail. He bent down and regathered it.

Unlike the rabbit he was stiff. The moisture had crept through to his skin hours ago as he slept. His sleep had been accidental, while he waited in the grass for a deer. When he woke with a shiver, he'd seen the rabbit grazing in the moonlight. All it took was two clicks, first the safety catch and then the trigger, and an instant later it was dead. He'd known it wasn't enough, but at least it was something. Now as he walked he felt ashamed of himself, for hiding away and surrendering so easily to sleep and the dreams it brought. He had neglected the children, letting them fend for themselves while he did nothing. Tomorrow he would bake bread and collect some honey from the hive. He'd drive out to Melton; perhaps he'd take them with him. He felt a sudden gratitude towards the contractors, for the release their arrival had brought. But there again came the shame, as he remembered standing before them with the rifle.

As always, he had dreamt as he slept. He'd seen the herd lying in the yard and in the barn. Thinking they were resting he'd moved among them, pleased at their apparent contentment. But then he saw how their tongues lolled from their mouths. Looking closer, he saw the awkwardness of their bodies, as if instead of settling they'd dropped where they stood. From somewhere came the regular crack of a rifle larger than his own. Then he was at the calf shed. Unbolting the door, he was surprised not to see a single head poking through the pens. Stepping inside, he wondered at the silence of the place. He looked down. There, running down the gutters built into the floor, two streams of blood. Strands of straw floated along with it.

His foot landed in a tramline and he came to with a jerk. The rifle strap slipped on his shoulder, the silencer nearly catching the back of his head. Shrugging it back into position he stood where he was. Suddenly weak, he felt the same numbness from before start to creep over his face. He set off again, tightening his grip on the rabbit as best he could.

The night wrapped itself around him, chilling the damp in his clothes. He heard the stubble brushing against his boots; it was harvest time. The soil's work was done, the crop it had harboured for all these months mature now and ready to be taken from it. It was time for the land to rest. He wondered if the farm would mourn the departure of the crop the same way it had seemed to mourn the loss of the herd. He thought of the ungrazed water-meadows, and of the empty barns. Finally he thought of himself, and the horrors he'd endured in the days that followed.

The numbness in his face was spreading. Then, without warning, the rifle slipped again. This time the strap fell to the crook of his arm before dropping to the ground. For a while he did nothing but stand over it, struggling to keep his balance. He found it was all he could do to coordinate his muscles. He didn't understand what was happening, couldn't comprehend why he couldn't simply bend down and pick up the rifle. His thoughts ran into one another; they flailed about as he tried to order them. By now more of him was numb, and he found himself wondering vaguely if it was winter, and if the stubble underfoot was really there at all.

Standing there, he did the only thing he seemed capable of. He breathed. The rifle forgotten, he tried to remember the way back to the farmhouse. Then, with a great effort, he turned and continued on, much slower now, his left foot dragging noisily over the stubble as he went.

12

The dawn came slowly. At first light a layer of mist hung about the farm, and to Billy it looked as if the earth and the sky were being stretched slowly apart after the unity of the night. Having witnessed the previous two daybreaks from his hiding place in the tyre, it seemed to him that the process was taking longer than usual. What he didn't know – in part because until now he'd only ever lived among streets, in part because he was only nine – was that up on the higher ground the farm buildings were already bathed in sunlight. Down here in the cool of the water-meadows the mist would take longer to shift. Not knowing this, and shivering with cold, he wondered if this time some of the sky had got stuck, if he'd have to spend the day walking around in a cloud that was either too heavy or too sleepy to rise any higher.

He'd spent much of the night remembering the heat of the day with the sort of affection he reserved nowadays for the airgun or his precious tin of WASPS. The way he remembered it – the all-encompassing warmth, the sensation that surely he would never be cold again as long as he lived – reminded him in turn of having a bath, and then it occurred to him that he hadn't had one of those for a while. The blackened rims of his fingernails were proof of that. Although small next to the old man's, it pleased him that in this respect at least they were alike. During the night, however, he'd become so cold that the prospect of a freshly run bath had hung tantalisingly before him. So far into his mind did this thought burrow that he began to believe that it was steam he was surrounded by instead of mist.

Soon after dawn some deer came past. They could only have been a few yards away – they had to have been or he wouldn't have seen them – but they never made a sound. He wondered if they were ghosts. Then he wondered if he was one too, if in fact he'd died when the machine hit him. Maybe that was why everything looked so different; maybe that was also why he was so cold. At one point one of the deer's ears pricked up, and it turned and looked at him. They stared each other. After a time it lowered its head and continued grazing. Perhaps I'm invisible too, thought Billy. Perhaps that's part of being dead. They moved away from him a step at a time, their shapes becoming wispier, their edges blurred, until one by one they disappeared into the mist. He remained as he was, looking at where they'd been long after they'd gone. His hand went to the back of his head. He flinched as his fingers moved over the stickiness.

He got to his feet. He was cold, but the hedge had kept off the worst of the damp. Brushing himself down he saw how the various twigs and stones had left their imprints in the bare skin of his legs. He'd never slept outside before, and because he'd spent much of the night awake he felt he'd witnessed things other people knew nothing about. There was the way the little birds continued to flit about in the hedge above him long after sunset; there was the constant creep of insects on the ground; and there was the strange scream he'd heard out in the meadow. The noise had scared him; for hours afterwards he'd lain there listening for it to come again.

He walked up the hedge now, and then out into the meadow. All he could see on the ground were the darker lines of green where something had cleared a path through the dew. Looking back he saw his own tracks leading away from him into the mist, back towards the hedge that he could no longer see. His trainers were already wet through. Suddenly feeling very alone, he followed his tracks until he was back where he'd started. His head throbbed from standing up, and he sat down in the little patch he'd cleared for himself and looked out at the greyness.

He didn't know what to do. He wasn't sure if he could

find his way back to the farmyard, and he wasn't sure if he was dead. For a time he stayed where he was, worrying that he might be. The memory of that day on the beach returned to him, of the cottage and the police station, and the way everyone's eyes had seemed so strange and empty. He remembered the funeral. He knew there was a connection between all of these things, but he didn't know what. He thought of the eggs and shivered. He didn't think they'd been eggs at all, yet still Jackson had sniffed hopefully at them. He'd watched as first the terrier licked them and then crunched them with his teeth, leaving drops of watery blood on the lino.

Pulling his knees up to his chest he wondered what, apart from being invisible and cold, being dead would be like. At some point he dozed off, and when he woke he thought he saw a figure slowly taking shape before him. It was his mother, and she was smiling at him. 'Billy, darling,' she said softly, 'are you really sure?' He stood up, and doing his best to get over his surprise he tried to think of an answer. But then she began to disappear, drifting away from him into the mist the same way the deer had done. It was only when she'd gone that he realised he didn't know what she'd meant. Sure about what? His head throbbed, and again he reached back and felt the stickiness with his fingers.

He decided to follow her. He walked and walked. After a while he found more dark lines in the grass where creatures – maybe deer, although some of the tracks looked very like his own – had been before. Occasionally he saw a shape up ahead and he slowed, treading as quietly as his sodden trainers would allow. But as he drew closer it turned out to be a red-topped thistle, or a clump of nettles. Spiders' webs hung draped about them, heavy with droplets of dew, like miniature strings of pearls. He stopped and poked them with his finger, mimicking the struggles of a fly. But either they were too laden with moisture for the spiders to sense his efforts, or the spiders themselves were waiting for the sun to rise, for none appeared, and he soon stopped trying.

As he continued on he thought of the other Spider, and the chase of the day before. He'd been crossing the yard when he saw the little man coming towards him. He ducked into the barn and looked about among the old machinery for somewhere to hide. He could hear Spider's footfalls coming closer, and before he could think what to do there he was behind him, framed against the brightness of the farmhouse beyond. He shouted something, and so the chase had begun, boy leading man on a hopscotch route through and around the farm buildings. Much the faster of the two, it didn't take long for Spider to come so close that Billy could hear the breath coming and going from his mouth. Even in his panic he imagined he could hear the concentration and anger in it. Never before had he been chased like this, and it was only when he squeezed through a gap in the wall by the old workshop and ran for the cover of the field of barley that he began to believe he might escape. He remembered how the moment he'd reached the crop he'd lain down, covering himself with the surrounding stalks as best he could. He'd waited. As he did so he pictured Spider standing by his chickens, looking out over the field, his fists clenched by his sides while his quick little eyes searched for the slightest movement.

Then came the noise, a roar like the one he'd heard that day on the beach. But instead of salt stinging his eyes, this time it was dust, and soon he couldn't see the ground in front of him. Desperate for air, he was on the verge of scrambling to his feet when something hard struck him from behind, catching him squarely across the back of the head. For the briefest of moments he was aware of his own surprise – and then nothing.

The slow *caaw-caaw-caaw-caaw* of a crow came from somewhere out in the mist. He stopped and glanced about, looking for it. He guessed it was then, when everything went black, that he'd died – so when he'd opened his eyes again and seen the giant shape of the machine lumbering away from him, spewing out straw in its wake, it had already happened. He scrunched up his eyes, confused by his own reasoning. If he really was dead, then why did his head hurt so much?

He opened his eyes; there, materialising out of the mist before him, was an oak tree. The slow *caaw-caaw-caaw-caaw* came again, and looking up at the higher branches he saw it. The crow was perched near the very top, its black shape easy to pick out against the whiteness. It tilted its head forward and he heard it again, and as he watched, the first rays of sunlight broke through, lighting up tree and bird as one.

13

'Come on, I won't bite.'

Grace pulled herself up the last few rungs. The feel of the metal in her hands reminded her of climbing the grain bin. She stepped inside the cab. Before she could sit down she had to wait for the man called Jimmy – the one who'd waved at her the day before, the same one who'd yelled at the old man to let them get on – to move his things. Once she was settled he reached past her to close the door, the hem of his shirt falling loosely over her knees in the cramped space. He smelt of deodorant. She inhaled, moved by the memories it stirred in her: first the boys' changing room at school, and then their bathroom at home in the morning after Michael had showered.

The door slammed shut, and it was suddenly quieter.

Jimmy reached about, flicking switches and carrying out checks. He brought the steering wheel forward, adjusting it until he was comfortable. The idle whirring of the engine behind them strengthened, and through the glass Grace saw Frank hear the change and turn towards them. He raised his hand, flicking a thumbs up, before turning back to the older man he'd been talking to, the one who Grace recognised from the previous night by the cigarette that dangled from his mouth. The combine lurched forward.

She thought of the rabbit. It had been waiting for her that morning at the bottom of the stairs. Beyond it the door into the garden had been open, and she'd stepped over the little corpse to close it. A handful of flies had blown off the creature's face and out into the early morning sun. She'd checked the kitchen and then the sitting room. The old man blinked at her from his chair. His trousers were wet around the ankles, and one side of his mouth was turned down. It made him look sad, and remembering the pile of newspapers upstairs she'd felt that she understood why. 'Billy didn't come home last night,' she said from the doorway. The old man's face didn't change; only Jackson seemed to take any notice of her, pricking his ears from where he lay at the old man's feet. 'I'm worried about him,' she went on, 'he's never not come back at night.' This time the old man grunted at her, a small sound that she took as a sign of his disinterest. She'd turned to go, but then she paused. 'I know about the herd,' she said, looking back at him. 'I know and

I'm sorry. I wish you'd told us.' The old man said nothing.

Back in the passageway she'd looked again at the rabbit. Its mouth and nose were partially covered by something dark, and she knew it must be dried blood. The one eye she could see was open; bits of dirt covered the pupil. She wondered what the old man meant to do with it. It occurred to her that it might be nothing to do with him, that Jackson might have caught it and brought it inside. She'd reached down and picked it up across its back. It was soft, much softer than she would ever have expected of a wild animal. But it was cold too, and stiff; its legs and head stayed fixed at the same exaggerated angles as she carried it through to the pantry. She laid it down on the floor as gently as if it was still alive.

Sitting down at the kitchen table she'd eaten a spoonful of honey. The sweetness was comforting, and as she ate her thoughts turned to Billy. She knew he had hiding places around the farm, and she guessed it was in one of these that he'd spent the night. She screwed the lid back on the jar and returned it to the cupboard. It was the last one they had left, and she wondered if she should hide it. It was something she'd considered before; it was one of Billy's peculiarities to want something someone else found precious rather than to want anything purely for himself. But Billy's not here, she'd said to herself, and as she sat there the silence around her had seemed to confirm it.

She left the farmhouse and began to search the buildings.

She expected at any minute to round a corner and see him creeping up on something, with the airgun held before him. She passed the blue Ford; two of its tyres sat flatly in the dust.

She was near the top of the yard when the men arrived. She watched them get out of the trucks and move across to the larger vehicles that they'd left there overnight. Only then did she remember what Frank had said the previous evening, about small boys and their fascination for harvesters. Her step quickened as she hurried towards them.

'Bit early for collecting eggs, isn't it?' Frank said when he saw her.

The other men's conversations paused as they glanced over at her. She was about to ask them if they'd seen Billy when she hesitated. Liz's smiling face sprang up in her mind, and there with it was the threat she posed. It surprised Grace even to think it, but she found herself wanting to protect their strange existence. However difficult or lonely their lives were here, in whatever weakened form the family had at least remained.

'Or have you come along for a ride?' said Frank.

Seeing there was another way to look for Billy, Grace nodded.

'Well, you'll need to hang around for a bit. We need to check everything, and then it's a waiting game. Sooner the sun burns off the dew the sooner we can get on. That's the check the boys are doing now. It's that automatic for us it's something we hardly even know we do any more, if you see what I mean. It's second nature. One morning, a few years back, when we were lifting spuds out at Brooke's, Keith found a fox asleep in his tractor, right there on his seat. He'd left the door open the night before to get the smell of his dinner out. That was a cold few days, and his missus had done him some soup, and he'd knocked his Thermos over. Old fox must've smelt it and got in for a look around, then decided on a bit of kip while he was in there. It was probably still warm from the engine. He come and got us, Keith did, and we all saw it. Old fox wasn't too pleased when he woke up and saw us lot standing there, gawping at him. Should've seen him go – bang,' he made a quick motion with his hand, 'gone, just like that. Cab stunk of fox all that day and the next.'

Grace remembered the fox she'd found, and how it had died in the night. She remembered the sharp smell, and the feel of its fur when she'd stroked it.

'There's that bearing that wants fitting, too,' continued Frank. 'And then we'll have our breakfast and get going. Saying that, you look like you could do with a good feed yourself. I don't know how you young girls do it, I really don't. I know that's the fashion these days, but,' he paused again, 'but that don't seem *right*, I suppose is what I mean.' He looked about. 'Where's your brother?'

'It's just me.'

'Well,' said Frank, raising his eyebrows. 'Well,' he said

205

again. 'There's a thing.' He shook his head, and then smiled at her. 'Right then. That's not often we have a girl riding along, but I don't suppose there's any harm in it. Only like I said before, that's better for us if you ask Mr Ambrose first. The last thing we want is to get wrong with him.'

'I already did.'

'Well, that's all right then. And don't you worry about Jimmy – he's not that bad really, underneath it all.' Standing a few yards away, Jimmy had heard his name mentioned and looked over at them. 'Looks like you've got company, Jim. So you mind your manners, and your language, especially. I don't want you turning the air blue in there with this young miss sat next to you.'

It was a tight squeeze getting out of the farmyard. Spider's chickens rushed about as the machine towered over them, its front wheels nearly as high as the fence that surrounded them.

'They yours?' said Jimmy.

Grace shook her head. 'They belong to a man called Spider.' She waited for him to laugh, but he only smiled. 'He gives us eggs though.'

'Think I saw the fella yesterday. Little guy, is he?'

Grace nodded, but then she wondered if it could have been Billy. 'Yes, but sort of old as well as small.'

'That's him. Come haring out of that end barn right in front of me, and then up here. I thought someone must be chasing him, you know, he looked to be moving that fast. But then he stopped up here and looked about, like he was lost or something.' He shook his head. 'Rum chap, by the look of him.'

'He's all right.'

She looked along the fence for his bicycle but it wasn't there. The memory of trying to find the village came to her again. The thought alone made her weary. The endless tarmac winding through fields, the sun reflecting up onto her legs as she worked the chain.

They soon reached the field they'd been harvesting the night before. Turning onto the stubble, Jimmy flicked some more switches, and then, as the combine lined up with the crop, Grace saw the broad front of serrated teeth on the header start up. She could hear them too as they sliced back and forth, snapping at the air. Gradually they lowered, disappearing into the barley. The tines turned above them, guiding the swathes of felled stalks onto the fast-spinning boom, which barrelled them inside the machine. All this she could see from where she sat. The movement was mesmerising, and she had to force herself to look away before she became too dizzy. By her side Jimmy sat hunched over the steering wheel, not missing a thing. He reminded her of the kestrels she'd seen around the farm, of the way they hovered, holding themselves perfectly still in mid-air as their eyes searched the ground below. He was so lost in his work that she found she was able to look at him properly. Beneath his baseball cap his clean-shaven face had a doughy look, the bones well covered. His skin was pale, much the palest of all the men. Above all, he looked clean.

'What's with you?'

Grace started, her cheeks colouring up.

'It's all right, no harm in looking,' he said. He turned his attention back to what was happening below them. He shook his head slowly a couple of times. 'No harm at all.'

There was a grinding noise, and Jimmy stopped the combine. He backed up, raising the header. The teeth at one end were covered in soil and straw.

'Fucking uneven ground,' he said under his breath. He tilted the header as far back as it would go, trying to get gravity to clear it for him. But it didn't. With quick annoyance he stopped the teeth and dropped the revs. Pushing the steering wheel up and out of the way, he stood up and made to come past Grace. She tried to move her legs out of his way, but still she felt the rough denim of his jeans as he opened the door. A rush of heat came into the cab, carrying with it the smell of freshly cut crop.

She watched him climb down and start clearing the soil with his hands. His energy reminded her of Spider, but he was more deliberate, more manly in the way he did things. She remembered the strange word the old man had used to describe Spider on their first day: hobbityhoy. 'Neither a man nor a boy,' he'd said afterwards, as if the way it rhymed gave it sense. Jimmy, on the other hand, was clearly a man. As she watched him work she felt envious of him, of his life as she imagined it. It was straightforward, untouched by confusion or unhappiness.

He climbed back up and pulled the door shut behind him. The smell of deodorant coming from him was stronger now, and as Grace watched him settle back into his seat she found herself wanting to reach over to him. But she didn't; instead the combine resumed its steady course up and down the field. She looked away and concentrated on scanning the margins of the field, hoping that what Frank had said was true, that she'd soon see Billy standing there, watching. She soon became accustomed to the beeping alarm that told them the tank was full. Tracking the combine up and down the field like nervous parents, the tractors took turns to come alongside and receive the grain. She saw the drivers behind the protective glass of their cabs; now and then they were swallowed up by the dust, the chaff hanging in the air all about them like a yellowy smoke, flickering here and there as it caught the sun. It looked hot out there, but inside she grew colder and colder, until her bare arms and legs were covered in goose bumps.

The combine shuddered to a standstill.

'Dinnertime,' said Jimmy.

He stood up and moved towards Grace, and then reached down beside her for his things. His face was inches from hers, and she leant forward and kissed him. For a moment everything was still in the cab, but when she kissed him again he seemed suddenly to come alive.

'I said there was no harm in looking, but this ...' He shook his head and frowned. 'How old are you? Fourteen, fifteen?' Grace said nothing. He shook his head again. 'I must be twice your age. And anyhow, I'm married. You can't go around kissing married men. What if my boss had seen us? What's he to think? I could be out of a job off the back of that.'

Not knowing what to say or do, Grace just sat there. Once more Jimmy reached for his things, only quicker this time. He straightened up and looked down at her.

'Come on,' he said, his voice softer. 'There's no need to look like that. Let's say no more about it.'

He opened the door. Outside, the heat chased the chill of the cab from Grace's skin, making her shiver. She followed Jimmy down the steps, and when she turned and looked she saw one of the tractors was parked alongside them. She heard the stubble cracking under the driver's feet as he walked towards them.

'All right, Jim.'

Jimmy nodded at him before settling down on the ground. He opened the Tupperware container he'd brought from the cab and Grace watched as he considered its contents. A memory came to her of a similar tub they'd kept biscuits in at home. Lynn had taught her how to remove the excess air by pressing down on the centre of the lid while holding one corner open a fraction. It kept the biscuits from going stale.

'You want a beer?' said the other man as he stood over them. 'I've got a couple under my seat.'

'What about Frank?'

'He's busy with that bailer again.'

Jimmy looked up, shielding his eyes from the sun with the peak of his cap. 'It still not working?' The man shook his head, and Jimmy did the same. 'Fucking thing.' He continued shaking his head. 'Fucking thing,' he said again.

'So – do you want one?'

Jimmy thought about it. 'No, better not, Carl. Maybe later.' He nodded towards the ground. 'Grab a seat.'

Carl sat down beside them. He looked at Grace and smiled at her. He was younger and taller than Jimmy, and his shirtsleeves were rolled up. His arms were muscular and nearly as tanned as hers.

The two men continued talking as they ate. Grace watched them hungrily. When they were finished they got to their feet, but when Grace did the same she stumbled. She felt strong hands catch her, and when she looked Carl was holding her.

'I'm okay,' she said, regaining her balance.

'You sure?' said Jimmy.

She nodded. He gave her his bottle of water and she took a mouthful.

'Course you've not eaten anything either, have you?' he

said, and opening the plastic tub under his arm he gave her a bar of chocolate. 'Get that down you.'

'Why don't I take her back to the yard?' said Carl.

'Good idea.' Jimmy looked at Grace. 'Carl'll run you back.' He paused. 'I expect you've seen enough of me today anyway.'

Still feeling dizzy, Grace nodded. Jimmy was soon back in the combine, and she watched it move off, the teeth lowering until the crop was falling before them once more. In her hand she felt the chocolate begin to soften. She pictured herself sitting in the cool of the farmhouse as she ate it. Perhaps Billy would be back. She promised herself that she would share it with him if he was.

Carl was waiting for her. A jet of diesel smoke plumed into the air, and the tractor started moving. She stood on Carl's left, hunched over beneath the low ceiling. When they hit the first tramline she nearly fell on top of him. The bar of chocolate spun to the floor. Steering with one hand he helped to steady her with the other, holding the waist of her denim shorts. She braced herself against the ceiling with her hands as best she could, her legs as far apart as the small space would allow as she tried to keep her balance. Looking down, she searched for the chocolate bar, trying to see past the pedals and Carl's legs and boots to where it had fallen.

Soon afterwards Carl's hand moved. At first she thought he was searching for a better grip, but then she felt it move from denim to skin. His fingers were warm and strong on

212

her thigh. She stayed as she was, unable to close her legs for fear of falling again. She looked through the glass and concentrated on the tractor's progress across the field. But after a short while his fingers moved again, this time finding their way under her shorts. She flinched, and as if encouraged by her reaction his touch became more purposeful. She held her breath, not knowing what to do. She wanted to move but her body had frozen, as if his fingers were some kind of deadly creature that would soon continue on its way. She found herself watching his other hand as it worked the steering wheel. It seemed the two were connected: there was the one she could see and the one she could only feel. But while the fingers on the steering wheel were smooth and certain in their movements, the ones between her legs touched and probed, as if searching for something they were unable to find.

The throaty drone of an engine reached the farmhouse. Slowly it began to penetrate the old man's mind. At the moment of recognition his breathing changed, and his grip on the chair tightened.

He saw a machine. It seemed to grow out of the noise, flowering yellow until he could see it clearly. It was a JCB. He watched it turn out of the farmyard and onto the track. He heard the pitch of its engine fall as the driver shifted gears. The sound of it grew fainter, receding into the distance.

He was alone. The farmyard was silent, so silent that it roared in his ears. He tried to turn away from it but it came at him from all angles, from the barns and the sheds to the trees and eaves all around. Nothing stirred: not a cow murmured, not a bird sang; even the insects were still.

He dared to look about. There, covering the concrete of the holding yard in a muddled terrain of black and white bodies, lay the milking herd. The dream shifted to the day it had happened. One of the animals blinked as he picked his way through them, and then began to struggle beneath the weight of the animal lying across it. She was still struggling when he returned with the rifle. He didn't need to see the number on her rump to recognise her, or to know how many times she'd calved. It was number 304. He found himself talking quietly, trying to calm her as she struggled, her eyes bulging. Seeing his fingers shake as he fiddled with the little brass cartridges, he knew he was trying to calm himself too. So far he hadn't been able to do anything for her – for any of them – but now he needed to be strong. Above all, he must be steady.

The magazine clip slotted into place. Setting his feet apart, one on either side of where a third animal's head lay stretched forward from the rest of its body, he readied himself. He brought the gun up and placed the muzzle close to the cow's forehead, between its staring eyes. He waited. As if knowing his intention she lay still, and with a final quick adjustment the old man pulled the trigger.

The bullet entered her head with a hollow crack. Her body shuddered, her front legs quivering before him, her hooves held off the ground. It was a small calibre rifle, too light by far for this job even at close range, and quickly working the bolt he shot her again. He needed to be sure. Blood started coming from the two small holes in her skull, and after a while she was still.

He raised his head and looked away. Everywhere he saw animals lying over each other. Even the buildings around him seemed to look on with disbelief, stunned by the scale of death laid out before them. He might have stayed like that for ever, might never have moved again, had he not seen a second cow stirring away to his right.

The dream switched back. In the distance he heard the JCB. It was days since the slaughter, and in all that time the birds had stayed quiet. But now, as he stood there, another sound filled the air. Countless flies moved over the carcasses, rising in great grey clouds before settling again. Already their eggs were hatching. He wished he could get away, wished he didn't have to stay to witness their work. But still he couldn't leave the herd. Why did they leave me like this? he wondered. Why did they leave me?

The JCB turned into the yard. The Land Rovers were back too, parked neatly beside each other. Men in protective white suits appeared out of the calf shed, dragging the smaller bodies behind them before throwing them onto an open-sided trailer. Then he was with them beside the pit. The trailer tipped up and the calves slid as one into the hole. Before it lowered again he saw the streaks of blood and urine across its base. He felt the heat from the flames on his face. The air was thick with the smell of burning hair and flesh. Then came the JCB, with more carcasses held aloft in its hydraulic jaws. He watched as the black and white shapes dropped into the pit. The flames leapt up to meet them.

In the sitting room of the farmhouse, one of the old man's legs kicked out, catching Jackson across his back. The terrier whimpered as he woke, raising his head and blinking sleepily. He nosed the old man's foot where it had settled on the carpet. Giving another whimper, he continued to nose him for a long time afterwards.

PART FOUR

14

Billy lowered his head to the water. At that angle the surface was glassy, and all across it he could see the hatch of pale flies. He lowered himself still further, until first his chin and then his lips met the water and were submerged. He opened his mouth, letting the water bubble into it. It was cold, colder than he'd expected, and he stayed as he was, feeling the chill spread over his tongue and between his teeth. His cheeks bulged from the pressure of the current, billowing in the flow. Finally, he drank.

The stream curved beneath the bank he was on, so that he was looking directly upriver. As he drank he imagined he was a part of the meadow, that the water was flowing through him, coursing in through his mouth and then filtering out through his fingers and toes. He could feel the chill right down to his stomach now. When he could manage no more, he lifted his head and pulled himself back up onto the bank.

He sat for a while, watching the flies on the surface again. Now and then the larger shape of a dragonfly appeared, its wings clattering noisily. Wondering if they might try to eat the smaller flies, he was disappointed when they ignored them. One landed close to him at the water's edge, and he was able to watch as it lowered its colourful abdomen under the surface. He saw its mouth and eyes, and the area on its back where its wings were attached. The shape of its wings reminded him of a hairclip of Grace's, but although this made him think of her, the memory of her prompted no more emotion in him than the memory of the hairclip itself. A moment later both were forgotten, as another dragonfly came downstream and landed on his foot. It flexed its body, and he imagined it was panting after the exertion of flight. Then it was gone, chasing the first dragonfly away across the meadow behind him.

He reached down and picked some watercress. He folded it up and put it into his mouth, and then lay back in the grass and chewed. It was a swan that had shown him it was edible. He'd seen it ripping at the leaves with its beak, and at once he'd recognised the bird's hunger. When it saw him and pushed itself away along the narrow band of water, he'd picked some of the same leaves and tried them. They were sharp, peppery in his throat, and made him cough if he had too much. But he'd liked them, and moreover he'd immediately felt better for eating them.

Although the visions of his mother had continued, he was now nearly certain that he wasn't dead. As well as hunger and thirst, he found he was at the mercy of the heat and cold just the same as before. Because of this he tried to make the hollow in the bottom of the hedge more comfortable. First he picked away all the stones and twigs he could find, and then he searched the meadow for something to lie on. Following the stream into a wood, he found a stand of bracken growing in the shade. He tried to snap the stems but discovered they would only bend and twist. Losing his temper, he pulled at them with all his strength, moving around them as he tried one angle and then the next. The stems split and sliced into his hands. He held them up before his face, looking with surprise at the ribbons of blood that ran from his palms. I must be alive, he thought to himself, quietly pleased. He sucked at the cuts, the taste of himself strange in his mouth. Suddenly Lynn was there beside him, and he held his hands out for her to see. 'I didn't know plants could be sharp,' he said aloud to her, but all she did was smile and say as she always did, 'Oh, Billy darling.'

When his cuts had dried he looked again at the bracken. He circled the plants carefully. It occurred to him that he might be able to strip the leafy side stems off the tough main stalk, and when he tried it he found he was right. He carried as much as he could back to the hedge. He crawled into the little space and laid the bundle of greenery out, covering the soil as evenly as possible. When he was done he stretched out on it: it was even more comfortable than he'd hoped. Encouraged, he returned to the wood for another armful. Back in the hedge he built up one end for a pillow. The rest he laid to one side, ready to be pulled over himself in the night if he was cold.

Despite having accepted that he was alive, he didn't think to return to the farm. The meadow was peaceful, and now that he had a den to sleep in, as well as food and water, it didn't cross his mind that he might want to be anywhere else. Whereas the farm had become a place of danger, pervaded by Spider's fury and the strange and deafening noises, the meadow was a place of sanctuary. Here he could do truly as he wished, with only his mother and the animals for company.

Grace kept a candle by her bed, letting it burn into the small hours. When she woke the shadows it threw frightened her, and she blew it out. Moments later she felt about for the matches and lit it again, already missing the comfort of the flame.

Earlier that day she'd run a bath every few hours, but instead of stretching out in it as she would normally, she'd sat upright and washed herself as quickly and thoroughly as she could. The stone-cold water was only part of the reason for this change. As well as this, where before she'd cherished those paler parts of herself, now she willed her tan to fade, so that the areas Carl had taken such an interest in would no longer be so clearly highlighted. In her mind there was now nothing left of the girl she had been before the accident on the beach: the last remaining traces of her had been eradicated. The reflection of herself in the bathroom mirror seemed dishonest to her, untrue in some way, and more than once she considered breaking the glass to be rid of it.

In the morning there was still no sign of Billy. Although nervous of the windows, she wandered from room to room as if she might find him hidden away in a cupboard, or tucked under a bed. The only room she avoided was the sitting room, in case the old man would know simply by looking at her what had happened. When she finally forced herself to go in there, it came almost as a relief to find him asleep in his chair. His beard was getting long, his hair too. Jackson lay at his feet; more than ever it occurred to her how much they looked alike.

On her way back past the front door she paused, halted by the memory of it. When they'd arrived back at the farmyard, Carl had turned the tractor into the shade of the big barn. Switching off the engine he'd pulled her onto his lap and started kissing her, his tongue alive in her mouth. When she resisted, he stopped and looked at her. 'What?' he said. 'I saw you in the cab with Jimmy. I know what you want. He's got a wife, but you don't have to worry about that with me.' Then he'd started kissing her again. Both his hands were moving over her, and when she gasped from the pain between her legs he'd clamped his mouth harder still over hers. It was then that she'd seen Spider standing beside the tractor. Their eyes met, and in that moment she imagined they shared a look of understanding. Then Carl saw him too. The two men stared at each other through the glass cab. Feeling his grip on her loosen, Grace pulled free and fumbled with the latch on the door. She scrambled down the steps and ran for it, heading past Spider towards the light and nearly falling because of her flip-flops. When she reached the farmhouse she slammed the door behind her and drew across the bolts.

Now she looked again at that same door. She pictured Billy standing outside, pushing against it before giving up and walking away. The thought made her catch her breath, and reaching out she slid the bolts back. But then came the panic, and she bolted it again. She leant against the wood, her head in her hands, not knowing what to do. A moment later Jackson was there next to her. He took a couple of steps towards the door and nosed the gap in the frame. She heard him exhale against the wood between breaths. She hesitated, struggling to think straight. Is it Billy he can smell? Or was it Carl? Again the panic rose in her.

When she finally opened the door she found neither. She stood there blinking in the brightness. The grass was browner than ever, and she felt the heat on her face. She looked about. Soon her gaze passed over that part of the lawn where she'd spent so many hours sunbathing; her stomach knotted as she remembered what else she'd done there. Although she did her best to resist it, she knew there was a connection between that and what Carl had done to her. His fingers and hers, there under her shorts. Their movement over those parts of her. And yet in her mind the two things were unrelated; her body too had seemed to know the difference.

She began to feel breathless in the heat. In the distance she could hear the sound of machines at work. Jackson reappeared from the long grass and came past her, trotting purposefully back down the corridor towards the sitting room. She looked about for Billy one last time and shut the door.

Back in the cool of the house she pictured the men fighting their battle against nature in their machines. She knew now she was on nature's side, not theirs. Mother Nature and me, she thought, two females together: they were the only ones. She was surprised she hadn't realised this before, but then she remembered: there was one other. She covered her face at the images the memory brought with it. It was Jenny, the donkey she'd watched being molested by her own son.

She retreated to her room. Later a syrupy smell reached the farmhouse. It came in through her bedroom window, hanging heavily in the humidity. When she looked she saw smoke over the barn roofs. She imagined it coming from the combine, rising up from all around as the dust had done; then she imagined it was a tractor that was ablaze. Inside she saw Carl, his face emotionless as the flames silently engulfed him.

She lay on her bed, worrying about Billy. She hoped he was nowhere near the fire. I should be out there looking for him, she thought, suddenly angry with herself, not hiding in here like this. But still she stayed in her room, while outside the sun moved over the farmhouse. Shadows turned and lengthened, before being gathered up by dusk. Determined to raise the old man from his chair, to make him understand that she needed him, she went down to the sitting room. But when she opened the door she found him exactly as before. 'Are you awake?' she said from the doorway, her voice sounding strange to her. There was no response. 'Please wake up,' she said, louder this time, 'I need you.' But still he sat there. She thought to go over and shake him, but something about the shape of him in the gloom frightened her, and once more she retreated to her room.

Later, as the night deepened, she heard the sound of vehicles leaving the yard. Lying there in the darkness, she saw there was nothing left to do. In the morning she would leave the farmhouse and find Frank. She'd tell him everything: about Billy, about the old man, and about what had happened with Carl.

Billy spent the heat of the day lying in his den, sleeping and waiting for the sun to drop. When the air cooled he crawled outside and, getting to his feet, he stretched the stiffness from his body. Before setting out across the meadow he raised his head and sniffed the air, catching the distant scent of smoke.

He headed to the stream for a drink. Afterwards he lay back in the grass, chewing and swallowing watercress a bit at a time. Later, he tried to catch the tiny fish that darted to and fro in the shallows, their sides reflecting the sun like strips of silver. Though he didn't think to eat them, something in him insisted that he try to contain these little creatures that moved about with such freedom. Despite his efforts they were too quick, or there was a gap between his fingers through which they escaped. But where before he might have grown annoyed and frustrated at his failure, now it was simply something that happened. Even the incident with the bracken and his cut hands he viewed without a hint of regret. He now had a comfortable place in which to sleep, and because of his cuts he would know what to do the next time.

He walked the meadow, creeping up on rabbits in the long grass. The hedge opposite his own grew along the top of a bank, and there in the sandy soil beneath he found their burrows. As he watched them disappear underground he wished more than anything that he could follow. Dropping to his hands and knees he put his head inside the larger holes and peered into the darkness. He liked the smoothness of the earth walls, and how it looked as if, were he small enough, he could tumble down into the ground. He pictured himself arriving in a big cavern far below, with rabbits lying all around.

He glanced up and saw a fox standing a few yards from him, its own head thrust into a hole. When it too looked up they stared at each other. It was so close he could see the amber of its eyes. He watched as it loped away along the hedge, stopping once to look back before climbing the bank and disappearing from view. Instinctively Billy followed, not wanting the encounter to be over so soon, and when he reached the top of the bank and wriggled through a gap in the hedge he found himself standing on a well-worn track. The grass was trampled and tired-looking. He tensed as another familiar smell reached him, one similar to the smoke he'd smelt earlier. There, flattened into the ground, he saw a cigarette end. Other unidentifiable smells competed for his attention, but instead of hunting about for their origins he turned and retraced his steps, his body hunched over as if he was trying to make himself as small as possible. Rabbits and fox forgotten, he crossed the meadow until he came to his den. There he stayed, unsettled by the smells that still lingered in his nostrils. Without knowing why, he decided never to climb the bank again.

That night the sky was so clear he felt certain there were more stars each time he looked. He imagined his mother there next to him, and they looked together. Lying on the bracken, he listened to the birds flitting about in the branches above him. He imagined them making their last-minute arrangements in readiness for daybreak. Already they seemed to have grown accustomed to him. In the daytime their only reaction to his movements was the briefest of pauses – and then their song would begin again. He liked watching them, and wondering at how such small creatures could be capable of such volume. Their effort at least was obvious: they stood as tall as they could on their chosen perches, their chests swelling with each intake of breath; then their beaks stretched wide as they returned that same air to the world laced with music. They appeared to be collectively looking forward to something, and in the absence of anything to look forward to himself, Billy tried to work out what it could be – if he found it, perhaps he could share in it. Then he remembered how he'd first woken in the meadow to find everything draped in a thick mist. The birds had been silent; only when the sun broke through had they finally stirred. Immediately he stopped worrying about having things to look forward to, and was only thankful when he emerged from the den and felt the sun warm on his back.

His T-shirt and shorts were becoming increasingly ripped and dirty. More than ever they fell baggily about him. Where before he hadn't paid much attention to his body, now he studied his arms and legs at length, running his finger over his skin and feeling the bone beneath. Far from being worried, he liked his newfound hardness; in his mind he associated it with a growing strength. Partly this was to do with the wound on his head: already it had become firmer to the touch, and less painful. He felt he had become lighter too, and this he also decided was a good thing. Everything around him was light, from the birds in the hedge to the fox and the deer that crossed the meadow with barely a sound. It was the deer that preoccupied him. At first when he'd tried following them, all he could do was watch as they dashed away from him across the meadow, leaping with athletic ease, flashing their white rumps in alarm. But now they too seemed accustomed to him, allowing him to trail behind at a distance. The only place he saw their footprints was in the softer ground by the stream; that they were bigger than him and yet left less evidence of their passing fascinated him. He tried walking on all fours as they did, but he found it to be slow and unnatural: even in the grass it was so obvious where he'd been that he soon gave up. Why is it only me that walks upright? he wondered. He thought of Spider's chickens, and of the two legs they walked around on. Was he more like a chicken than a deer? The idea annoyed him, and thinking of the chickens made him remember the eggs he'd stolen. He pushed all of it from his mind.

Alone in the meadow, he quickly came to know silence as his own. His thoughts began to slow to match his breathing, and he soon found he could manage not to think at all. All that remained was the sensation of his breath as it came and went. Then only a sudden gust of wind or the shriek of a jay could disturb him. Though he hadn't slept, he'd blink himself back into consciousness, looking about as he wondered how long he'd been there. Afterwards he felt happier than he could remember being, and not knowing why only added to it.

Next came the dizziness. It started slowly, his vision speckling out when he stood up. When it happened he waited; usually it didn't last for long, and then the meadow would gradually come back into view. Occasionally it didn't pass so easily and he was forced to sit down. Although these episodes didn't worry him, he did wonder why they happened, and if there might be something wrong with him. At no point did he make the connection between dizziness and a lack of food. Once, he fell asleep where he sat, waking some time later under the sun, his mouth dry and his head pounding. Picking himself up, he made his way to the stream and rested there awhile, drinking and chewing the peppery leaves. He splashed water over himself in an attempt to wake up before trying to decide what to do next.

Grace left the farmhouse early. She'd lain awake for much of the night thinking it through. Again and again she reached the same conclusion: that she no longer had any choice. Even the prospect of Liz, along with all that she represented, seemed less of a threat now. She knew she needed help. And despite her fears about running into Carl, her acceptance of this brought its own relief.

The safest way, she'd decided, was to wait out of sight near the top of the yard. From there she could watch the men arrive, and only when she saw Frank would she make her move. She looked about anxiously for Billy as she went, keeping to the cover of the buildings. What was he eating? She remembered her own breakfast of a few minutes ago, sitting at the kitchen table as she listened for any signs of movement from the old man. None came. Something smelt bad, and she'd opened the fridge. A whitish fur grew on some of the shelves; otherwise it was empty and sour smelling. Closing it she'd returned to the table and finished what was left of the bread and honey.

When she reached the top of the yard she knew at once that something was wrong. Even so, it took her a few moments to realise what it was. Where the machines had been there were only bits of straw, and here and there on the concrete handfuls of spilt grain.

She stood still for a while. She felt sick. Perhaps they're already out in the fields, she thought hopefully, and she kept walking. She listened for the machines, but the only sound came from the stubble under her feet and the cooing of doves from the barns behind her. When she reached the next field she saw where the fire had been. The ground was black with ash; whole ears of barley lay all around. She felt dismayed at the sight of it, knowing for certain now that the men had gone. She looked again at the blackness, saddened by how a field of living crop could be turned into such ugliness.

In the distance she saw the propellers of the wind turbines. From where she stood they looked like giant spurs, urging the clouds on. Never before had she felt so alone. A shape out in the middle of the field caught her eye. She paused, shrinking from the idea that it might be Billy. By the time she reached it her feet were black. She looked down at the shape before her, seeing it was nothing more than a clump of greener crop. It lay low against the ground, as if shielding itself against sun and fire alike. Gradually, her heart slowed.

She continued on, following the lines of hedges that had contained the fire until she came to a gate that led into the next field, and then the next. She saw the tracks from the machines in each of them, dual lines that weaved between the straw bales. She started calling Billy's name, but unused to such activity her voice soon grew hoarse, and she was forced to stop. She walked and walked. The sun climbed higher overhead, and in the heat she began to see the hopelessness of it.

By the time she returned the farmhouse she was tired and hungry. Stepping into the kitchen, she saw three or four small shapes moving quickly over the table. One after another they trickled down one of the wooden legs like little dark droplets, before crossing the lino and disappearing from view. She looked closer at where they'd been, at the remaining crumbs from her breakfast.

She moved towards the sink, keeping half an eye out for any quick little shapes that might appear around her feet. When she passed the stove she reached out to touch it. It was cold. She shook her head, the slight daze she was in deepening as she wondered how she'd be able to cook anything. Then she saw the telephone on the shelf beside it, and again she shook her head, amazed that she hadn't thought of it before. But even as she handed it down she wondered who she could call; all her numbers had been in her mobile phone. She lifted the receiver and listened. Hearing nothing she replaced it and tried again. Nothing.

She began to circle the room, her eyes roaming over everything as she looked for anything that might contain food. The smell from earlier seemed to have strengthened, and when she opened the door into the pantry a stench rose to meet her. She could hear flies buzzing in the darkness, and when she tried the light switch part of her was glad that it didn't work. She closed the door, remembering the rabbit.

She was about to give up her search when a tin on the top shelf of the dresser caught her eye. Pulling a chair over she climbed up and brought it down. It was half full of seeds, and she recognised them from the bread the old man had made. She picked out a couple – a sunflower seed and another she didn't know – and popped them into her mouth. They were dry, but there was just enough softness at their centres for her to know that it counted as food. She sat down on the chair and ate another couple while she tried to work out what to do.

Leaving the kitchen, she walked along the corridor to the sitting room. She paused, and then pushed open the door. A buzzing sound came from the window. A dozen or so flies were on the glass; intermittently one of them would lose patience, blurring into a tiny ball as it tumbled down the pane. The old man sat in his chair, exactly as before; Jackson too was in his usual spot at his feet. The terrier looked up at her with his brown, expressionless eyes as she came nearer. Her hand was nearly on the old man's shoulder when a movement caught her eye. It took her by surprise, and she jumped back, thinking that he'd woken. But when she looked nothing had changed: still he slept. Then it happened again, only this time she saw it. A single strand of cobweb, shifting fractionally in response to her own movements. It ran from his left ear to the rim of the lampshade on the table beside him. And, as she watched, a bluebottle crawled out of his nose.

15

Billy sat in his den, listening to the children's voices. He could see them from where he was: they were on the bank by the stream, the two adults sitting with the two children playing beside them. They'd come across the meadow from the track above the hedge. He'd been returning with a fresh armload of bracken when he saw the sun reflecting against the brightness of their clothes. The blues and reds and whites were so unfamiliar to him that he'd dropped instantly to the ground. He'd stayed there, watching them through the grass. From somewhere nearby came the alarmed chatter of a blackbird. He was confused by their presence. What did they want? When he was sure they hadn't seen him he began to slither towards the hedge, parting the grass with his hands and using his legs to propel himself slowly forwards. It was an exhausting process, and stopping to rest at regular periods it was some time before he reached his den.

The sound of laughter prompted strange feelings in him. With it came a memory of another time, of children running and playing together on hard ground, surrounded by wire and all wearing the same clothes. He knew it was his old school he was remembering, Maddox Primary, and that one of the children was him. Similar thoughts ran through his head when he looked at the two children over by the stream, and the grown-ups that were with them. There was something familiar about the scene, a sense that he might have been one of them once, too. But instead of wishing himself back to that time, all he wanted was for them not to be there, for the meadow to return to how it had been before.

He watched them for a while longer, before lying down and trying to sleep. But he couldn't: the sound of the children wormed its way into his brain, stirring up more memories of his old life. He found himself picturing his teachers as he dozed, each of them frowning or looking disapproving in some way. Then he saw the object of their displeasure. It was himself. He was standing before them, wearing his uniform. When he saw how unhappy he looked he wanted to rush over and shield his younger self from their eyes. What did they know about anything? Did they know how to live in a meadow, or how to make a den and a bed out of bracken? Had they ever tasted those peppery leaves that grew alongside the stream, or the berries in the hedge that sometimes made you sick? Of course they hadn't. All they did was sit in a classroom all day and talk about words and numbers. What use were words and numbers when you were following deer though the grass? Being able to count them didn't change anything, nor did knowing how many fish were in the stream help get them into your hands. And who cared how words were spelt? You didn't need to know how to spell to live in a meadow; with no one to hear you, you didn't even need to speak. Why didn't they teach us about the different birdsongs instead? he thought, or the smell a fox left behind? I could have used things like that. I could have shown Lynn what I'd learnt, I could have pointed out which animals were which and where they liked to sleep.

A scream and then a splash echoed across the meadow. One of the children had fallen in and was being helped back onto the bank. The child's laughter filtered into Billy's thoughts, until he sat up, all attempts at sleep gone now. Clambering out of the den, he straightened up and stood by the hedge. They hadn't seen him. He began to walk across the meadow, and when he was some ten yards from them he wondered if perhaps it was only the animals that could see him. But as he drew closer the woman reached out and touched the man. They stood up; together they watched him approach. The man whispered something that Billy couldn't hear, and the woman turned and spoke to the two children. Her voice reached him across the grass. 'Emma, Sam, come here. No, leave that there, Sam, you can't bring it with you.

Good boy, that's it.' He heard the fear in her voice and wondered what it was that she was frightened of.

The man took a step forwards, moving to one side so that his wife and children were behind him. He was tall, with curly hair cut short. He wore a short-sleeved shirt, which was open at the neck. His watch flashed gold and silver under the sun.

'Hello,' he said. Transfixed by his watch, Billy ignored him. The only thing in the meadow that glittered like that was water, yet here was this man wearing the sun on his wrist. He wanted to touch it, but when he raised his hand and reached towards it the man drew away from him, tucking both his arms behind his back. Only then did he look up at his face.

'Hello,' said the man again. He smiled encouragingly. 'What's your name?'

'Ask him if he's by himself,' whispered the woman behind him.

'Of course he's by himself,' hissed the man back at her over his shoulder. 'Look at the state of him.'

Billy shook his head. 'I'm not. By myself, I mean. There's rabbits underground and deer in the mornings and evenings and all the birds in the hedge. And Lynn's here too, sometimes.' He stood there, blinking with surprise at his easy fluency, at the sound and rhythm of the sentences.

'Who's Lynn?' asked the man. 'Is she your mother?'

A small voice piped up before he could answer. It was the

girl. 'Daddy,' she said, peering around the side of his trousers, 'what's wrong with him? Why's he all bony and dirty like that? Is he hurt?'

'Shush a minute,' said the woman, taking hold of the girl by the shoulders and trying to prevent her from looking. But she struggled free, and resumed her position by her father's leg. The boy, who Billy saw was younger than both him and the girl, was also watching, his eyes wide. Billy looked back at the girl. Her hair was curly like her father's, but fair and long, so that it hung down in loose ringlets. The two of them looked at each other for a while, until the girl said to no one in particular, 'I don't think he has a mummy. If he does, she's not a very good one.'

'Emma!' said the woman. The girl glanced at Billy, checking for his reaction, as if he was an animal she'd just prodded with a stick.

'I do have a mother,' said Billy, 'and this is where we live.' He looked at the man and then around at the rest of them, even at the boy who had begun to cry. Seeing other people was nicer than he'd thought it would be, and although standing there under the sun was making his head spin he felt a glow of pleasure at their company. 'You can stay here too if you want,' he said. 'There's lots of room, and you've already found the water and the pepper leaves. There's berries too, but—'

'You can't live here,' said the man. 'There aren't any houses.'

'Joe—' started the woman.

'Hang on.' He raised his hand to silence her. 'I'm just trying to find out what's going on here.'

He began to look Billy over, starting with his nest of tangled hair and moving down over his ripped T-shirt and shorts. Next came his knees, bulging out of his skin as if they belonged to someone much larger than himself, and then there were his bone-thin calves that were covered in all manner of scratches and bruises. When he reached his trainers, which had all but fallen apart, he worked his way back up again. All the while the young boy's crying grew slowly louder behind him, his back turned to this horrible creature that had appeared out of nowhere over the grass and spoilt their afternoon.

'So where's your mother now?' said the man.

Billy said nothing. He knew there was a connection between the little boy's crying and the way the man had looked at him, but in his light-headedness he couldn't place it. The different strands of thought curled and twisted before him, running parallel to each other but never quite meeting. With a final effort, during which his eyes scrunched up as they often did at such moments, he managed to push the strands together into a single entity – and there it was, suddenly clear to see, and he understood. For days now the only creatures to have seen him were the animals in the meadow. Sometimes he'd wondered what they thought of him: did his uprightness puzzle them just as their ability to walk on all fours had confused him? Did they think his T-shirt and shorts were extra layers of loose skin that were as much a part of him as his arms or feet? And if so, were they amazed on those occasions when he took them off and jumped naked into the stream? Since coming to the meadow, these were the aspects of his appearance that had occupied him; but now, as he stood before this man and his family, another memory of how things had been before jerked into being. He opened his eyes and saw again the way the man was looking at him. He saw the same thing in the girl's face, and then, with a surge of sadness, in the woman's too. Their displeasure at the way he looked was obvious; even the little boy, he realised, was crying because of him. Glancing down he saw himself afresh, from his ruined clothes to the streaks of dried mud on his legs. A feeling he hadn't felt since coming to the farm moved through him, and he found he wanted to cry, to hide his face like the little boy was doing and bawl it out of himself. They hadn't known him for more than a few minutes, yet already they were looking at him as if they wished he was different.

'Your mother,' said the man again, enunciating carefully as if he suspected Billy's brain was as ragged as his clothes. 'Where is she now?'

Billy looked away. All the pleasure he'd found in their company was gone. His eyes flitted to and fro, before settling on the sandy bank in the near distance. He concentrated on it, picturing the rabbits underground, safely out of reach. The man and the woman began to talk among themselves, in that way Billy now remembered adults did. Had he listened he might have known what was coming. 'We *have* to,' the woman was saying, 'he's nothing but a bag of bones. Look how he's swaying all over the place – he's hardly the strength to stand.' 'But what do we—' began the man. 'Please, Joe. Imagine he was yours and someone found him. You wouldn't want them to leave him there, would you?'

But Billy heard none of it. And so, when the man stepped forward and took hold of his arm, saying, 'Come on then, lad,' in a voice softer than before, he immediately pulled away, staring at him with surprise. The man tried again. This time he was more insistent, less easy to evade; and now something changed in Billy too. Instead of pulling away as before, he threw himself angrily forward.

16

Grace woke with a start. Her sleep had been fitful: she'd dreamt it was Billy lying there in the pantry, the flies moving over his face, coming and going from his nose and mouth.

The air in the room was fresher, and the curtains were shifting in a breeze. Briefly her memory was obscured by the damp, pregnant scent of rain, but then she thought of the old man in his chair, and of Jackson at his feet. She wondered why the dog would stay there if it were true. She began to think that she'd been mistaken about the bluebottle; but then she remembered the cobweb, and she knew.

She got up and went over to the window. She was still dressed, and in her pocket she anxiously fingered the remaining seeds, turning them over faster and faster, feeling how smooth their skins had become under her touch. She closed her eyes, calmed by the breeze as it moved over her unwashed skin. When she looked again she saw a bank of cloud to the west, coal-black and moving towards the farm like an advancing tide. The first drops came, streaking the open window; and then, coming in a rush over the rooftops and thudding audibly into the ground below, there it was. The sky darkened, and soon everything with a surface glistened wet. The larger flints and pebbles on the ground winked up at her. To start with the dust around them resisted the change, but the weight of water was too much, and it was soon making the transition to mud. Grace reached out with her hand, as if not quite trusting her eyes and needing to touch to really believe. Even seeing it there, cool and clear on her skin, wasn't enough, and she bent down to taste it.

Returning to her bed she thought again of the old man. That his life could have ebbed from him so quietly made her scared for her own: who was to say that one of these times when she drifted off she might not wake again? She remembered how she'd felt after Lynn and Michael had died, that the moment should have been marked by a change in the things around her. She knew now that she'd been wrong to expect it. She thought of all the rats and doves that Billy had killed around the farm, and how all there was to show for it were dried bones and empty nests. She thought of the old man's cows and their hoof marks in the track past the paddock. She thought of Jackson, still lying at the old man's feet.

The sound of rain grew fainter. The curtains ceased their movement; a short while later rays of sunshine broke through and lit up the room. She imagined Billy watching the rain with wonder just as she had. Perhaps if he'd been caught out in it he would be cold, and finally he'd return to the shelter of the farmhouse. Other less pleasant possibilities occurred to her, ones that involved the machines and the fire in the fields. The image of flies moving over his face returned to her.

She realised something as she lay there. If I don't move from here, if I never leave this bed, no one will ever know. The world will continue without me. She thought of the old man and wondered when it had happened. She remembered how he'd blinked at her when she told him about Billy. That was the last time she could be sure he'd been alive. Had he been dead when she asked him to help her? And then it struck her: there was a dead body downstairs. Her heart raced at the horror of it. She wondered why he'd died: he'd stopped eating – perhaps that was it. Remembering the cold stove in the kitchen, she tried to think how long a person could go without food. She took a couple of seeds from her pocket and ate them, trying not to panic as she thought of herself lying slumped in her bed, the same as the old man in his chair.

Without warning she began to cry. She cried for her parents and her home, and for Billy and the old man. Now she had truly lost everything. Soon, she thought, as well as everything else, any fat I had will be gone, leaving only my bones and my tendons and my muscles. I'll be reduced to my limbs and my organs, and my blood besides; and then, at last, there'll be nothing left to do but die.

For a time Billy was able to kick and bite and scratch as best he could. Seeing his teeth sink into her husband's thigh, the woman gave a shriek and edged backwards, taking her two children with her. This time the girl went willingly, her prodding curiosity replaced by fear. With shock giving way to pain, the man caught hold of one of Billy's wrists. He let go again as he felt the bone break in his grip and shift under the skin.

Billy sprang back. His other hand moved instinctively to the break, and clasping it against his chest he turned and ran. He didn't get far before the dizziness came, and he slowed to an irregular jog. Behind him he could hear the woman shouting at the man to follow, to catch him before he got away. The man shouted something back at her that he couldn't hear, his voice drowned out by the howling wails that now came from both children.

He never looked back. Even as light spots began to appear before his eyes he had enough sense left in him to wait until he was out of sight on the other side of the hedge before cutting along it towards his den. When he reached it he stretched out on the bracken and panted like an exhausted animal. He listened for any signs of pursuit. None came. Later – much later – the last thing he would remember doing was sitting up and peering through the undergrowth across the meadow to see if they were still there.

When he woke, most of the light had gone from the sky. The meadow was silent, the leaves still in the trees. He lay there for a time with his eyes closed, feeling his wrist throb with each heartbeat. He tried to remember what had happened. Much of it was vague, the order of events muddled. Had the man attacked him? He wasn't sure; he knew they'd fought, but why? The tiniest details lodged themselves in his mind, obscuring the bigger picture – like the man's watch and the girl's blonde ringlets, both of them glinting in the sun. And then he remembered: there was the way the man had looked at him, and what the girl had said about him not having a mother. He shifted at the memory of their disapproval.

He fell asleep again and dreamt of his old bedroom, with the stripy curtains that had at one time matched his pyjamas. There too was his cabin bed, with the inbuilt drawers beneath and the high edge all around that was designed to stop him rolling out in his sleep. His parents were standing in the doorway; he saw their frowns as they discussed him in hushed tones. Then a girl was standing beside them, but instead of Grace it was the girl from the meadow. His parents didn't seem to have noticed, and when he tried to tell them their frowns deepened. It was only when he started to cry that Lynn came over to him. 'Oh, Billy darling,' she said as she sat down and held him, 'whatever are we going to do with you?'

He woke again when he rolled onto his wrist. A sudden sharpness jabbed at him, yanking him from his sleep. He thought an animal had crept into the den and was biting him, and he quickly pulled his wrist out of its reach. The pieces of bone jarred against each other, and he nearly passed out from the pain.

He lifted his head and examined the damage. The area around the break was swollen and discoloured; the mix of blues and greens and browns looked like some kind of liquid that might burst through his skin at any moment. Narrow beams of sunlight were coming through the foliage above him, and he realised it was day again. He looked about, staring through the leaves at the brightness. He wondered how long he'd been there.

The wind picked up, and before long the sky went dark. He heard the rain before he saw it: it swept over the grass towards the hedge, and soon drops of water were working their way through the branches towards him. He must have drifted off again because when he woke the sky was bright, the clouds gone. He heard voices in the meadow. Listening, he wondered if he'd dreamt it all: the conversation with the man, the struggle – had he never even left the den? Had he dozed off while listening to those children? But then came the throb from his wrist.

The voices grew louder. He knew at once that it wasn't the family from before: this time there was only the deeper sound of men's voices, without the punctuation of laughter. Soon they were so close he could feel their footfalls, could hear the swish of grass against their shoes. Snippets of conversation reached him, their voices too similar for him to tell how many there were. 'Like a wild thing,' he heard, 'you could hardly believe it was human ... something to do with the travellers ... didn't stop crying till we got him home.' Then he saw them: three men, one of them the man from before. They were walking yards from the den. As he watched they came closer, before stopping and standing around together while the man pointed one way and then another. His voice rang out clearly.

'I said to Susan, I said, "What'll we do if we catch him? Lock him in the car? And then what? We can't very well put Emma and Sam in there with him, can we? Who knows what he might do to them. No," I said, "let's report it to the police and let them deal with it." And all the damn time the little ones are crying their heads off, they're so frightened.' One of the other two men murmured something, and then the man turned and looked towards the hedge, his hands on his hips. 'I don't know,' he said, blowing out his cheeks, 'I suppose he could just be a runaway, starved half to death. He could be from anywhere. He might be hiding up and watching us even as we stand here.'

Billy held his breath as the man looked straight at him. He imagined his own eyes as a pair of twinkling lights among the foliage, the two things that might give him away. He wanted to close them, to hide as much of himself as he could, but he worried that if he did the man would see the lights go out and know he was there for sure. He willed the branches around the den to come to his aid, to thicken and sprout more leaves; or better still, maybe the ground could open up and let him crawl inside.

The man turned away. He saw the way his shoulders rose and fell as he took a breath. Then the three of them were walking again, criss-crossing the meadow away from him.

He lowered his head onto the bracken. His heart felt large inside him; his whole body seemed to move with every beat. For a long time he lay there listening to it. When it was nearly dark he crept over the meadow to the stream to drink some water and eat some watercress. He held his broken wrist against his chest, fighting the dizziness that came and went. Back in the den he lay down with his eyes shut, feeling a little better after the water. He waited to drift off, hoping that he might see Lynn again, either sitting there next to him on the bracken or beside him on his old bed as he'd dreamt before. But the pain from his wrist drove any trace of sleep away.

As the hours passed his mind began to clear. He found he was able to pick over what had happened in the meadow more easily, to pluck out individual moments as they occurred to him, as if the conveyor that carried his thoughts had finally slowed. He pictured the man and his family asleep in their house. He imagined them waking in the morning, and seeing each other for the first time of the day. He remembered the man's expression when he'd caught hold of his arm. Something about it reminded him of the animals in the meadow: when he'd first come here they'd looked at him like that too. As if he was dangerous. By now the birds and the deer knew better: they lived their lives and let him live his in the hedge next to them. But it would be different with the man. He'd attacked him, he'd bitten him; he'd proved him right to be wary. Because of this, something had changed. Already he'd returned with two others to look for him. And what would they do if they found him?

The old world of schools and cars and adults loomed before him, of plates and carpets and toothpaste. But he couldn't go back; there was no one to go back to. He wished that Lynn was there, to prove that here in the meadow he wasn't alone. Thinking it might encourage her to come, he tried to remember how her hand had felt on his face when she brushed the hair from his eyes, or when she rubbed the tears from his cheeks with her thumbs. But he couldn't remember. It was only as the night deepened and she still hadn't come that he started to see things as they really were. The realisation, when at last it happened, knocked the breath from him, and he had to whisper it aloud to himself before he was able even to cry. 'She's gone,' he said, his voice tiny in the darkness. 'She's gone.'

17

Downstairs Grace moved about cautiously, going nowhere near the sitting room. The smell from the pantry had grown stronger, filling the kitchen from floor to ceiling. It hung draped over the table and chairs; it wrapped itself around her as she stood there.

She stepped outside. The sky had cleared, and she recognised the vibration in the air as the heat returned. Birds flew back and forth from the trees to the roof above her, where they drank from the gutters. She listened in vain for the sound of the machines, and then walked up the yard to where they had been. The concrete area was as empty as it had been before: there were only doves, which took off when they saw her. Their wing beats echoed in the barns, and she found herself wishing she could fly as they did, could swoop between buildings and over fields until she spotted Billy below. She stood still for a while, imagining she was with them as they circled above – and only then did she think of the grain bin.

It took all the strength she had to make the climb. She sat at the top, breathing hard, knowing she must eat something soon. She looked around: the burnt field stood out among the others, and as before she saw the reflection of the stream in the distant meadows. She scanned the buildings around her. Seeing the chimneys of the farmhouse, it shocked her again to think of her grandfather lying dead inside it.

She'd only been on the ground a short time when Spider appeared. She wondered why she hadn't seen him from the grain bin. He shifted from foot to foot as he always did, his eyes moving quickly around. She searched his face, but found nothing that reflected the moment they'd shared in the barn with Carl.

He reached out and took her hand. 'Sky today,' he said. He placed an egg into her palm. It was a blue one. So that's why I didn't see him, she thought. He was in the hen-house. 'Sky today,' he said again, 'maybe straw tomorrow.' He hesitated. 'But maybe sky tomorrow too.' He looked at her and then back at her hand, and when she didn't move he began to try to close her fingers around the egg. She pulled away, unnerved by his touch, but now that she had hold of the egg his face creased with pleasure. Satisfied, he turned and began walking back towards the chicken run.

She called after him, but he didn't seem to hear. She hurried to catch up. By the time she did he'd reached his bicycle.

'I need you to help me,' she said. He frowned at her. 'I need you to tell someone about the old man, about my grandfather.' Still he frowned. 'Mr Ambrose,' she said. 'He's dead. Do you understand?'

For a time neither of them moved. Then Spider started to nod.

'His cattle's dead,' he said. 'Big 'uns and little 'uns, all dead 'uns. In fire and out smoke.' He looked up. 'Turned sky to dirty water.' He pointed at her hand that held the egg and his face brightened. 'But sky today. Maybe sky tomorrow too. Or maybe straw.'

'No,' said Grace, '*he's* dead.' She didn't know how else to say it; if she could only show him the old man in his chair then he couldn't fail to understand. As it was he only looked at her with those narrow eyes before taking hold of his bicycle. He swung a leg over and pushed himself off in one quick movement, and then began pedalling away from her.

'Wait!' said Grace. She broke into a jog to keep up with him. 'You have to help me, I need—'

But it was no good. There was only the creaking of the chain and the rattle of mudguards as he accelerated down the yard, and when he rounded the corner onto the drive these too were gone.

She stumbled to a halt. She pictured him cycling along lanes until he arrived home. He lived with his mother, the old man had said, and now Grace pictured her as an old lady, something like the old man only tiny like her son. She wondered if she even knew that she and Billy were here. The thought made her feel so weak that she nearly had to sit down.

She looked at the egg in her hand. It seemed more perfect to her than anything she'd seen before, from the way it filled her palm to the smoothness of its shell. Sky today, she thought, knowing Spider had meant only that it was blue.

Back in the farmhouse she placed her hand on the stove. It was still cold. It struck her as strangely useless, as irrelevant as a tap without water. She sat down at the table, thinking what to do. The air was thick; dozens of flies stalked the window-panes, and she was soon on her feet again. Still clutching the egg, she looked around. This isn't a room for cooking and eating, she thought, not any more.

Fetching a frying pan from beneath the sink and a wooden spoon from a stoneware pot, she took them and the egg outside. Back inside she climbed the stairs, returning with the matches from her room. Then, with a handful of kindling from inside the porch, she prepared to make a fire. Hunched over the criss-crossed pieces of wood she nearly smiled at the sight of the first flames. Soon the wood crackled and spat, and adding larger pieces all the time it wasn't long before she felt the heat on her face. Despite her hunger she felt a reluctance to crack the egg, but then she watched as the white took shape around the yolk. A minute later she spooned it into her mouth, and all too soon it was gone. Her stomach seemed to gape in response, as if by eating she'd only made it aware of its own emptiness. She decided she wanted another – *needed* another – and almost before she knew what she was doing she'd left the farmhouse and was halfway up the yard.

The chickens raised their heads when she entered the run, and as they watched her open the door to the hen-house and disappear inside. Like Billy before her she searched the laying troughs by touch, her hands moving over the hay, her fingers feeling for the familiar shapes in the gloom. But there was nothing, not even one of the china eggs her brother had found before.

She heard a shrieking sound coming from outside; it lasted for several seconds and then came to an abrupt halt. The chickens were clucking with alarm, and when she stepped out of the hen-house and looked she saw Jackson standing over a pile of feathers on the concrete area. Glancing at the gate she saw she'd left it open.

She walked over to him. The chicken lay on the ground before him. He ignored her as she approached, continuing to rip at the bird's breast with his mouth. But when she reached down to take it from him, he froze. A low growl came from his throat. She tried to push him away but his jaws were locked shut; taking hold of the bird's legs she tried pulling instead, but without loosening his grip he pulled back. For a while they faced each other. She was surprised by her reaction to the sight of the dead bird, by the desire to chew and swallow that it prompted in her. 'Fair enough,' she said in the end, straightening up. 'You caught it, so I suppose it's yours to eat.'

She watched as Jackson continued to tear at the bird. It was some time before he stopped, and when he did he walked stiffly away. She stood over the carcass for a while, unsure. The bird's head was missing, and one side of its breastbone was visible from where he'd ripped the feathers and flesh away. The other side was untouched. Already flies were on it, and they continued to buzz about as she reached down and felt the remaining meat with her fingers. It was hard to tell how much there was through all the feathers, and before she knew it she was pulling them away in clumps with her thumb and forefinger. The skin came away with them when she tried pulling too many at once, but working patiently she was soon faced with a bald area that looked vaguely like the chickens she'd seen in supermarkets. But it was still attached to the rest of the bird, to the legs and the wings and the neck.

She picked it up and carried it to the farmhouse. Leaving it in the grass she went inside to find a knife, emerging moments later to see with relief that Jackson hadn't reclaimed his prize. There was less blood than she expected. Nevertheless, there was something unsettling about cutting a section out of a creature that had been alive only minutes ago, with the intention of eating it. During the process her hunger gradually receded, but she urged herself on, telling herself that this was the way nature intended it, that she was simply taking her place in the food chain. And anyway, she reasoned, I might have left the gate open but it wasn't me who killed it.

The fire still had some heat in it, and it wasn't long before the fresh wood took. She cooked the chicken breast in some oil from the kitchen, and then ate it so fast that she burnt her tongue. The meat tasted strong, but already she sensed the good it was doing her.

She sat on the ground beside the dwindling fire, leaning against the wall of the farmhouse. She closed her eyes, feeling the sun on her face. She heard a noise, and there next to her she saw Jackson licking the remains of the oil from the frying pan. Every now and then he paused and shook his head, making exaggerated movements with his tongue before licking again.

Sitting there, her stomach heavy from the meat, she began to see that nothing was the same for long. Where before she'd been hungry, now she was full; yet she knew that later or tomorrow, again she would want to eat. It was in everything: there was the sun that rose and set every morning and evening, and the ground that for so long had been dry and now was wet. She thought of the chicken, and of the egg it had started out as. Every moment since then it had been changing, hatching and feeding and growing until the time of its death. Even now it was undergoing changes, as parts of it were plucked and eaten. Next would come the work of the maggots as the flies' eggs hatched, until gradually, eventually, it would pass into nothing.

She cast about, applying her new knowledge elsewhere. Wherever she looked it was true: even the grief she felt for Lynn and Michael was changing shape into something that was easier to bear. She pictured the old man slumped in his chair on the other side of the wall she was leaning on. For years he'd lived here on the farm, but now change had come to him as well. And then there was Billy. He might be missing now, but that too will change. It has to.

She got to her feet, buoyed by this thought and the food she'd eaten. As before she began her search in the buildings, before taking to the fields. Drops of rain flicked up from the hollow stems of the stubble and onto her legs as she walked. When she came to the next field, she saw again where the fire had been. The ash was wet now and already beginning to mix with the soil below. She saw the first shoots among the blackness. She bent down and looked closer at the split grains, glad to her heart see this further proof of constant change, to see new life rising out of ground she'd previously considered ruined and ugly. As she continued on, something else settled in her mind. She was a creature of the land, and that land could feed her. This is a farm, she thought; this is why the old man was here. 'There's plenty of things that don't want buying,' he'd said to her on their first morning here. 'Plenty you can eat, and plenty you can make.'

She began to look about with fresh eyes. Whenever she came across them she collected berries and nuts from trees, tucking them into the upturned hem of her T-shirt. She even stopped to pick some pale mushrooms she found growing beneath an oak tree.

For two hours she walked like this. Not knowing quite how to search for Billy – should she look out in the open fields or in the woods; was he more likely to be in the sun or the shade? – once again she took to calling out his name. But as before her voice soon became husky, and she found she called his name less and less.

By the time she returned to the farmhouse her T-shirt was full, the cotton stained in places from her load. Clearing the kitchen table she laid everything out on the wooden surface, her disappointment in not finding Billy eased by the sight of it. She stood back and ran her eye over it all. Each individual thing seemed to hold the secret of itself hidden beneath its skin or outer casing; how, she wondered, am I to know what I can and can't eat? The old man would have known for sure. Perhaps taste alone will tell me what I need to know; perhaps sweetness and bitterness can be my guides.

She remembered the books upstairs, the ones she'd passed over so readily because of their titles. Fetching them down she pored over them, seeking out their wisdom. In ten minutes she learnt more about trees than she'd ever thought possible. But the news wasn't always good: neither the acorns nor the conkers were edible. She was surprised to find that the strange spiky clusters she'd brought back were – or at least the sweet chestnuts inside them would be if she could get at them. But when at last she managed to prise one open with a knife she was disappointed to find thin, anaemic-looking things that were nothing like the picture in the book. She checked the text: 'Fruit season October onwards,' it read. I'm too early, she thought, looking down at them again. These are just babies.

She carried on, working her way through books until she found an illustration or description that matched what she'd collected. She found the process strangely calming, and she realised how much she'd missed the nourishment of learning. She came to the mushrooms: 'Edibility: Excellent'. Some of the berries were good too. She began to get glimpses of the connection between all these things: the trees outside and their fruit laid out on the wooden table before her; the paper of the pages and the knowledge printed on them. These glimpses came as moments of startling clarity, and in among everything she saw herself, her own role no more or less important than any other.

All the while the smell from the pantry nagged at her. No longer able to ignore it, she went over to the door and looked inside. There was just enough light to make out the shape of the rabbit on the floor. It was hard to believe that it had once been something alive, that it had run and eaten and breathed just as she did. She picked it up and carried it out-side. She laid it down in the grass, seeing how the maggots had hollowed it out, and how there was so much less of it than there had been before. And where were those missing bits now? She thought of the flies on the window-panes in the kitchen, and returning inside she undid the latches and pushed them open. A strange satisfaction moved through her as she watched them fly away. It was a sense that she'd enabled some kind of cycle to complete itself, and it pleased her.

She felt a decision starting to form in her head, a growing knowledge of what she must do. She walked along the cor-ridor to the sitting room. Inside, the air shook with the weight of flies. The smell from the kitchen seemed to have followed her there, and keeping her eyes only on the things she needed to see she crossed the room and undid the latches on the windows. She threw them open. Fresh air drifted in; with it came the sound of birdsong and leaves shifting in the breeze. There, she thought, that's the best I can do. I may not be able to carry him out and lay him in the grass, but at least this way some of him will find its way out there.

She turned to leave, but couldn't resist taking one last look before she went. He seemed a different shape from before, more spread out across the chair. There was a move-ment beneath his shirt, and she quickly looked away. There at his feet, lying in his usual place, was Jackson. She tried calling him, but all he did was look up at her. Feathers were stuck to his mouth and nose. She called him again but still he stayed. Reaching down she picked him up, and holding him close she left the room, closing the door firmly behind her as she went.

18

The flock of doves ate greedily, picking and pecking at the ground as they worked their way over it. A pair of wood-pigeons passed overhead before circling around and dropping in to join them. The markings on their feathers held the brightness of youth; their beaks too were still soft and pliable, proof that they weren't long from the nest.

Later they turned into the wind and took off, one after the other. They climbed higher and higher until the doves disappeared from view; and now as they flew, hedges and trees shaped and mapped the land below. They soon came to the farm buildings, and the two birds dipped and set their wings, dropping down onto the railings of one of the grain bins. They ruffled their feathers, rearranging themselves after the exertion of flight.

A noise made them look up, their eyes rapidly seeking out its source. A car held their attention as it turned into the farmyard. It pulled up, and one of the doors opened. A red-haired woman stepped out and approached the farmhouse. She walked along the wall towards the door, but when she passed the window she stopped and looked in. For some time she stayed as she was, staring into the house. But what she couldn't see, and the pigeons could, was the tanned girl with hair that reached halfway down her back. She was running, past the grazing donkeys, past the beehive, and into the fields beyond.

PART FIVE

19

The car swept along the lane, its surfaces bright and hard under the sun. The long grass seemed to draw back as it approached, before relaxing again once it had passed. A haze of dust and pollen hung in its wake, an earthy vapour trail that thickened the air. Through it flew insects of all sizes, each momentarily thrown off course by the sudden commotion.

Grace saw none of this. From her position in the back seat she was aware only of the sweep and curve of the vehicle's movements, and the quiet hum of its engine. When she looked out of the window the glare hurt her eyes, and she soon turned away again.

She thought of the farm. Reaching forward, she scratched the raised bumps on her legs. She wondered why she'd run, why she'd been so desperate to hide. She remembered how she'd crawled in among the long grass beside an old wooden gate, hardly noticing the stings of the nettles that also grew there. All the time she'd imagined Liz pursuing her, but when at last her breathing had slowed and she listened, she'd heard only birdsong. Next to her, clinging to one of the longer stems of grass, had been a ladybird. It seemed to pause, to watch her as she was watching it. Then, a little at a time, it continued its ascent, following the length of grass until it reached the very tip.

She'd stayed like that until dusk. She must have fallen asleep because she dreamt she heard a dog barking, and there coming across the field was Jackson and the old man. It was dark when she was woken by a voice. She opened her eyes to find a policeman and his Alsatian standing over her; still half asleep, the panting of the dog had frightened her. The policeman had been holding a torch, and now as she sat there she wondered if that had been the flash of white she'd seen in her dream, the darting, running shape she'd thought was Jackson.

Again she wondered why she'd run. The sight of Liz walking up the yard should have come as a relief: here at last was an end to it, here at last was the help she needed to find Billy. Yet all she'd wanted was to be away from that woman. She pictured her walking into the empty farmhouse; perhaps Jackson had kept her at bay for a time, but eventually she must have found herself standing in the sitting room, looking down at the old man.

She stopped scratching her stings and leant back, too tired to imagine how Liz might have reacted. Instead, she wondered at her lack of urgency. Why, when she'd told her that Billy was missing, had she still insisted that they leave the farm and drive to the hospital? 'But there's nothing wrong with me,' Grace had said. 'Don't you get it? Billy's *missing*. He's been gone for days – it's him you should be worrying about, not me.' 'We have to go,' Liz had said without looking at her. She'd opened the car door and motioned for her to get in. 'Come on, quickly now.'

She shut her eyes and pictured the farmhouse. Already the sun would be high over her spot in the grass, and after their morning song the birds would be seeking out their places in the shade. She wondered if Spider had been yet today, and if he'd know that she'd gone. But then perhaps it was because of him that Liz had come in the first place; perhaps he'd understood what she'd told him about the old man after all.

When she woke she felt they were going slower than before. Outside she saw cars and houses, and streetlights and shops. She saw people walking on the pavements; still others waited at bus-stops. She stared through the glass at them, not knowing what to make of it all. And then she realised: this was why she'd run. It was on the farm that she'd begun to understand the way of things; just as the old man had died, so she had learnt to live. Out of all the difficulty of the past weeks had come the beginnings of a new kind of certainty, both in herself and the world around her. But now, as she looked through the window, she felt sure of very little.

She sat back on the seat and thought of Billy. Then came the itch from her stings, and she reached forward to scratch them.

20

Billy lay with his eyes shut, pulling at whatever it was on his arm. He wanted to reach over and push it off with his other hand, but when he tried to lift it he found he couldn't. It was wrapped in something hard and heavy.

He didn't know how he'd got there. The last thing he remembered was having to sit down in the grass on his way back from the stream; darkness had edged in over his eyes, and the next thing he knew he was surrounded by all this whiteness. He managed to lift his lids a fraction. Yes, everything was so white and hard. Rectangles and squares were all around him: above him the sky was framed within straight lines, and instead of being circular the sun appeared like a cube of light in the near distance. He wondered what could have happened. Perhaps this time I really have died, he thought.

He pulled again with his arm. He felt a hand on his shoulder, and a female voice spoke close to his ear. 'Careful, now. Just try to relax.' He tried to look to see who it was, the hope rising in him that maybe it was Lynn, but he couldn't focus. All he got was an impression of more whiteness. He closed his eyes, tired from the effort. He heard more voices talking, this time further away from him. For a time he listened, trying to make out what they were saying, but soon the gentle rise and fall of their conversation lulled him back to sleep.

When he woke later and opened his eyes, things were clearer than before. He saw he was lying in a bed in a room. The cubic sun was a window in the far wall. He looked around, confused by the murmur of conversation and a bitter smell he didn't recognise. It needled its way into him: he felt it in his nose when he breathed in, and then in his throat and down to his lungs. He felt sick because of it, and he retched dryly where he lay. The convulsions made his eyes water; by the time he laid his head back again the tears were running out of them. He tried to stop but they kept coming. One by one he heard them landing on the pillow beside him.

A little later a woman came and sat with him. This time he knew it wasn't Lynn, and he didn't bother to hide his disappointment. He turned his head away from her as she spoke, hearing her explain about the bag of liquid that hung above him. A thin tube ran down from it into his unbroken arm; it would make him well again, she said. He thought of the stream in the meadow, of the water rushing by and how he'd open his mouth and let it flow into him. Perhaps this was like that, he thought.

The woman started asking him questions. She reminded him of the man he'd attacked, the one who had worn the sun on his wrist. He had asked questions like this too. He thought of his den in the hedge, and the fox and the deer and the rabbits. The woman tried other questions, and when he still didn't reply she asked them again, her voice softer. He said nothing. After a while she seemed to get bored, and standing up she went over to the doorway. When she came back her voice had changed, and he realised at once that it was Grace. He looked at her, unsure, thinking that perhaps he was back at the farmhouse.

She sat down beside him, her hand on his, but soon her shoulders started shaking, and she stood up and went away again. Some time later she returned. 'Oh Billy,' she whispered, squeezing his hand. Immediately he felt the tears on his cheeks, and again he heard them drop onto the pillow. After a while they stopped and, reaching over, Grace wiped the last of them away.

She stayed until the woman from before came and told her she had to go. When she'd gone the nausea returned, and he looked across at the window. It was shut, but there on one side, out past all the whiteness, he could see the green of some leaves. Now and again they shifted back and forth, and sometimes when they did the light reflected against their paler undersides. From where he lay they looked like the only things alive, and for a long time he concentrated on them.

TO BE SUNG UNDERWATER

Tom McNeal

'For you, I was a chapter – a good chapter maybe, or even your favorite chapter, but, still, just a chapter – and for me, you were the book.'

Judith Whitman believes in the sort of love that 'picks you up in Akron, Ohio, and sets you down in Rio de Janeiro'. But she married more pragmatically.

Before her marriage to a banker, before her career as a film editor in Los Angeles, Judith was 17 and living in Nebraska, where she met Willy Blunt, a carpenter whose pale blue eyes and easy smile awakened in Judith the reckless girl he alone imagined her to be. Marrying Willy seemed a natural thing to promise. But a violent episode followed by acceptance to a prestigious university carried Judith away.

Twenty years later, Judith's sturdy-seeming marriage is suddenly hazy with secrets, and her thoughts drift back to the time when she and Willy had escaped to a small world where sunlight seemed always to fall from a softer angle. What happens now when she holds in her hand the number for the man who believed it, long ago, when she declared her love?

'You don't so much read *To Be Sung Underwater* as you're consumed by it. The characters are unforgettable. The writing is staggering. More importantly, though, it's the courage of this book that sets it apart. It's the bravest, most beautiful book I've read in a long time'
Marcus Zusak, author of *The Book Thief*

978-0-349-12363-9

A MISSING SHADE
OF BLUE

Jennifer Erdal

When translator Edgar Logan arrives from his home in Paris to work
in Edinburgh he anticipates a period of enlightenment and calm.
But with a chance meeting with the philosopher Harry Sanderson and
his captivating artist wife, Edgar's meticulously circumscribed life is
suddenly propelled into drama and crisis. Drawn into the Sandersons'
troubled marriage, Edgar must confront both his own deepest fears from
the past and his present growing attraction to the beguiling Carrie.

Moving, witty and wise, *The Missing Shade of Blue* is a compelling
portrait of the modern condition, from the absence of faith to the
scourge of sexual jealousy and the elusive nature of happiness.

'Deep waters and dense themes, marshalled with a
light touch and dry wit. Elegant, humane'
Guardian

'Absorbing . . . This is a writer of rare assurance and intelligence'
Cressida Connolly, *Spectator*

978-1-408-70375-5

Now you can order superb titles directly from Abacus

☐ To Be Sung Underwater	Tom McNeal	£8.99
☐ A Missing Shade of Blue	Jennifer Erdal	£12.99

The prices shown above are correct at time of going to press. However, the publishers reserve the right to increase prices on covers from those previously advertised, without further notice.

──────────── ⟨ABACUS⟩ ────────────

Please allow for postage and packing: **Free UK delivery.**
Europe: add 25% of retail price; Rest of World: 45% of retail price.

To order any of the above or any other Abacus titles, please call our credit card orderline or fill in this coupon and send/fax it to:

Abacus, PO Box 121, Kettering, Northants NN14 4ZQ
Fax: 01832 733076   Tel: 01832 737526
Email: aspenhouse@FSBDial.co.uk

☐ I enclose a UK bank cheque made payable to Abacus for £ . . . .

☐ Please charge £ . . . . to my Visa/Delta/Maestro

☐☐☐☐☐☐☐☐☐☐☐☐☐☐☐☐☐☐

Expiry Date ☐☐☐☐   Maestro Issue No. ☐☐

NAME (BLOCK LETTERS please) . . . .

ADDRESS . . . .

. . . .

. . . .

Postcode . . . . Telephone . . . .

Signature . . . .

Please allow 28 days for delivery within the UK. Offer subject to price and availability.